"Jo Lloyd has drawn out all the intensity and latent power of short fiction. All her effects are earned, and she writes with the assurance of an original mind. Line by line, her judgment is impeccable, and the whole has a substance and finesse that marks a major talent."

—HILARY MANTEL, THE *WOLF HALL* TRILOGY

"Jo Lloyd writes stories that have the epic sweep, sly humor, and cold, thrilling depths of Mavis Gallant and Jim Shepard, as well as an idiosyncratic brilliance that is hers alone. Her sentences could rouse the dead (and do, in this excellent book)."

—KAREN RUSSELL, *ORANGE WORLD*

"*Something Wonderful* is a wonder, and establishes Jo Lloyd as one of the best short story writers around. Each story here is a richly imagined universe, full of lush detail, human wisdom, and both humor and devastation. She bends space and time, leaping through generations in a few pages, or making a single interaction echo through a lifetime. This is an entertaining, masterful collection from a writer with awe-inspiring range."

—CAITLIN HORROCKS, *LIFE AMONG THE TERRANAUTS*

"A language unsettling and of terrible beauty. These stories are startling and wise, all-knowing and versed in the infinite variation of human folly."

—MATTHEW NEILL NULL, *ALLEGHENY FRONT*

Something Wonderful

JO LLOYD

 TIN HOUSE / Portland, Oregon

Copyright © by Jo Lloyd 2021

All rights reserved. No part of this book may be used or reproduced in any manner whatsoever without written permission from the publisher except in the case of brief quotations embodied in critical articles or reviews. For information, contact Tin House, 2617 NW Thurman St., Portland, OR 97210.

Published by Tin House, Portland, Oregon

Distributed by W. W. Norton & Company

Library of Congress Cataloging-in-Publication Data

Names: Lloyd, Jo, author.
Title: Something wonderful : stories / Jo Lloyd.
Description: Portland, Oregon : Tin House, 2021.
Identifiers: LCCN 2021019390 | ISBN 9781951142728 (hardcover) | ISBN 9781951142803 (ebook)
Subjects: LCGFT: Short stories.
Classification: LCC PR6112.L68 S66 2021 | DDC 823/.92--dc23
LC record available at https://lccn.loc.gov/2021019390

First US Edition 2021
Printed in the USA

www.tinhouse.com

FOR BARBARA AND ALAN

———————

After sunset, there are the lights, fixed, flashing, coloured, and white, in place of the prospect which night has blotted out.

Contents

My Bonny

James

L ESS than a year into their marriage, James—who had always, in his brief visits ashore, been tilted and clumsy, startling every four hours to interior bells, twitching to get back to the harbour and slide out on the falling tide with not one look, not even one thought for his loved ones left at home (You will be sorry, Agnes, her mother had told her, if you marry a man with clean fingernails)—passed over the visible edge of the world a final time and was lost (not, as it turned out, completely lost), his ship gone down far out to sea, witnessed only by spider crabs and hagfish and other untalkative actuaries of the deep.

Agnes would not marry again. John, not yet six months old, would be her first and last child. She would live another sixty-eight years a widow, sixty-eight years of relentless, erosive work, the cuckoo hunger gaping in her ribs. Had she known this when they came to her door with their heads bare and their eyes sideways, she might have knelt on the fire and waited for death, as widows were said to do in more fragrant corners of the Empire.

Both native to this Scottish port, they had been living, since their marriage, in a narrow cottage on the north side of its harbour. A good spot to watch the boats come and go, James always said. To watch the storms sweeping in, Agnes said. To see the waves blooming above the breakwater, the tattered sails of spray hanging in the air. The small boats staggering like crane flies, the ships listing and turning, helpless as leaves in a weir. The silent processions winding up the hill.

James would laugh, tease, finally lose patience. He remarked only those who made it through. The seven pulled from the water when the packet ran aground. (Sixty lost, Agnes said.) The master of the *Simeena*, saved within sight of the harbour. (And the rest of her crew drowned.) James held the sun's unquestioning belief in his return. As if wind and sea wove a downy pallet that he could nestle into, safe as the kingfisher's brood. When he was away, Agnes would try on his faith, pull it over her head like his Sunday shirt. She tried to imagine him fixed and solid among the flying ropes and scurrying men. The wind broke on his broad face, cleaved north and south of him, combing his hair smooth. His mouth was white with salt, his eyebrows frosted. He narrowed his eyes to the east, looking for Goteborg or Riga, Helsingor, Konigsberg, Drammen.

She preferred to render the watery section of his journey negligible. His destination lay just below the horizon, and the ship was even now safely tied up among surly Norwegians or Balts or Russians, the crew packing her holds with flax and timber and hides and thick black balsam spiced with aniseed and tar. After days of stacking and stowing, there would be another quick voyage, the moon pressing a pale track into the water, the waves humming sweetly. If Agnes stood a little straighter, if she went up the hill a short way, she might be able to spy the tops of the masts.

James had gone to sea as a boy of twelve. Back then, he had told her, he would watch for the long smudge of pearly cloud that would gradually clump and fray to reveal the moors behind the town, then the tower of the ruined abbey, then the smaller spires of churches and the low streets beneath them. Now, after twenty years of industry and innovation, of the harvests of the Empire flowing in and out of the harbour, the first thing he saw would be a wintery forest of tall chimneys. So many chimneys—a new one each time he came home, it seemed—marking the very flax mills and jute mills, the sailcloth and rope factories that his cargo would feed. The chimneys reached higher than the church spires, higher even than the abbey tower. From every one, smoke streamed straight up, then bent and set in thick, grey horizontals across the town, like a hundred signposts pointing in the same direction, as if just over there, out of sight, was something wonderful.

Stewart

Stewart Doig, master and, on that morning, sole crew of the fishing boat *Clio*, was idling towards shore, dwelling on the recent death of his mother, which had brought to mind also the more distant death of his father, and the sermons addressing this subject that he had sat through, sometimes dozing, sometimes thinking about fish, and what he had nonetheless garnered of death and burial and that surely still far-off day when the graves would crack and the saved would come forth riotous and laughing like a holiday parade (Would they be clothed in flesh, he kept wondering, or would they be just shinbones and clavicles and broken-toothed skulls?), when the body that had been James bumped at the *Clio*'s hull, sodden and swollen, as if in dark answer to Doig's questions.

Wrecks were common. Every winter there were four or five on the Great Rock alone. Dozens on all the reefs and sandbanks and rocky shores around the coast, dozens more in deep water. James was one of hundreds who drowned during that year of 1829, whalers, soldiers, fishermen, a whole consignment of convicts, cooks, doctors, farmers, labourers, emigrants and immigrants and deportees, men and women and children and pigs and sheep and cats and rats and dogs. The unexplained fate of James's ship—swamped by a freak wave, consumed by fire, holed by a rock or a vengeful kraken—was common, too, even in the increasingly crowded shipping lanes of the Pax Britannica. The sea was a veritable soup of dead people, whispering sedition and blasphemy and wrapping their cold fingers around the fisherman's heavy nets.

The body floated face down, and Doig had no reason to suppose it was the boy two years his junior that he had once pinched and pulled and knocked to the ground until James grew tall and stout enough to break young Stewart's nose. What he did know was that it would be twice the weight of a body on land, unwieldy, waterlogged, slippery.

He thought of his mother, how her face shrank in the instant of death and her mouth fell open as if in surprise.

By the time the thing was hauled over the transom, Stewart's hands were nearly as white and bloodless as it was. When it landed, he recognised James, even without the eyes. They had seen, perhaps, too much horror to come back to this upper world. Or been taken. There were other signs on the face and hands that needy parishioners below had profited from the occasion. Doig drew a piece of sacking over the head, as if to show respect, and put up all the sail he dared.

It was time, he thought, to leave the sea. Enterprises were springing up all over town: boatyards, mills, foundries. He would take a wife. There were new widows aplenty in the port this week, handsome young widows who knew how to keep a good house and look the other way when it was called for. Not James's widow, her waist still thick from the child dragging round her neck. No, he would choose a woman free of encumbrances, with a sweet figure and laughing eyes, and enough put aside to set up a man in his new life ashore.

Euphemia

By a combination of intelligence, thrift, and reluctance to bestir so much as one finger except to her own immediate advantage, Euphemia Symon had kept the small general grocery on Muir Street for three decades, first with her husband, and then without. After his death, she had a low upholstered chair carried into a corner of the shop, and there she sat, comforting herself with liquorice and coconut ice, sugared almonds and candied violets. As the years went by, Euphemia expanded to fill the chair and gradually to spill over its edges. Sugar draped crystalline, frosty webs across her memory, so that the details of her earlier life softened and receded. She found fault with the girls nowadays, who were no better than they should be, marrying too young and squandering their pennies on collars and China tea, with the wives who skimped on mending and with those whose husbands wore patched clothes, with the mothers who kept their children in school and with those who sent them out into the blighted sea fogs of autumn to risk scarlet fever, whooping cough, and measles (the disease to which, some twenty-five years earlier, she had lost both her children in the space of a week).

Euphemia was James's cousin by marriage. He had been a man poor in relatives, at least local ones, so when she heard of his death she expected his relicts to turn up, and so they did. Agnes, with the baby thrashing in her arms, stumbled through routine flatteries and pleadings, while Euphemia, not mentioning the very recent departure in disgrace of her moon-eyed maid-of-all-work, looked the pair over. She listened to the child's furious roars and thought it unlikely to be struck down by any of the thousand poxes. She saw that Agnes, although short, was sturdy and determined. She judged her not so pleasing as to distract the gentlemen, nor so displeasing as to tire a mistress's eyes. With a happy synergy of kinship, charity, and economic considerations, she offered Agnes a roof and employment.

Agnes scrubbed, swept, swilled, roasted, carried, boiled, rinsed, scoured, emptied, mended, scalded, blacked, starched, polished, while Euphemia sat in her corner, offering occasional advice or criticism. You are fortunate, she told Agnes often, and no one would have disagreed, even as Agnes's heart withered like a rosehip. In Euphemia's own veins, small threads of remembrance wormed forth and then burst, and she knew this, too, was fortunate.

Euphemia took a special interest in John. He had the same broad face as his father, the same far-sighted blue eyes, even— one would swear—the same tilt to his walk. She would tempt him with sugar mice and marzipan pigs, and as he stood at her knee with sticky face and fingers, she would tell him about the press gangs that ranged up and down the coast when she was young, parents hiding their children in trunks and cellars and pot cupboards. She told him the fates of the boys who were taken, of those, more foolish, who ran away to sea. The beatings, the sickness, the stench, the never-ending work, the dry tack soaked in coffee until the weevils formed a scummy layer on top (John testing with his tongue the melting nose of a pig). The boys who crashed from rigging to deck or had their bones peeled clean by chains and ropes or were ground like meat between boat and dock. The boys who died, the boys whose bodies were twisted to cages of pain so that they begged for death.

She described the death of his father, which she had seen for herself in the bare acidic reaches of the night. The groans and shudders of the vessel, the planks folding underfoot, icy water waist- then neck-high, men sliding unstoppable through the splintered decks, cursing and screaming and then silenced as the ship, like an overturned cathedral, plummeted into glacial blackness. Up on the surface, the unlucky few who had jumped or fallen clear floated for an hour or more in the moonlight, calling to each other, their limbs growing first cold then insensate, their voices failing as beside them, dripping salt and phosphorescence, rose monsters with the faces of angels and huge, uncurious eyes.

If Agnes disliked Euphemia's idea of education she did not say so. She took John to the sailcloth factory at the age of nine. If John had other ambitions he did not voice them, remaining silent through the transaction and afterwards taking up his new responsibilities without protest.

When Euphemia died, Agnes was fortunate again, quickly finding employment in the newest flax mill, and a room for her and John in the shadow of its chimney. The wind and the rain seemed to visit that corner of town with especial interest. Agnes slept with her hands over her ears. Sometimes she still dreamed, as she had since she was a child, that the sea did not stop at high tide but kept rising up the hill, until it lay all around in a rippling, hushed mass. This time, she thought every time, it is not a dream.

John

The people of the port raised their eyebrows over John, shook their heads. He spoke English as if it were foreign to him, went through his days widdershins. He would loom up without warning, like a hearth ghost, then be gone again, even while you were looking at him.

Where he went, alone and unnegotiated, was along the cliffs, over the beaches, up into the moors behind the town. He scrabbled down rocky valleys to the sea, clambered into caves and gullies, scaled bluffs and crags, waded through streams and becks and slacks and pools. He collected feathers, birds' eggs, skulls and leg bones, claws, teeth, mermaids' purses, the spiny pink carapaces of crabs, shells curled protectively around their moonlit inner floors. He sat in the rain for so long that they exchanged properties, his cohesion for its gleam, its velocity for his resistance, to form a new element, silvery and glutinous. He breathed through his skin, the water beading on his brows and lashes, fattening and trembling and finally spilling in heavy, white drops that rolled down his face and fell to the shingle, displacing the small arthropods that mined the intertidal zone. Invisible, he watched plovers, knots, goldeneye, skuas, redshank bobbing their anxious heads, oystercatchers, kittiwakes, ospreys, otters, porpoises, seals. Up on the moors, partridge, grouse, chats, ouzels, merlins, hare, deer, owls, ptarmigan, eagles with wings longer than he was. And in the cold, black tarns between the highest ridges, divers in their funerary best, singing the tuneless songs of the dead.

By 1841, the year of Euphemia's passing, he had been working three years at the sailcloth factory and would soon graduate to a full twelve-hour day, six days a week. Already, the times when he could wander were rare. He saw the sea more often by night than day. In the darkness it was a deeper darkness, a black pelt rolling beneath the stars. Even above the noise of the mills, he heard its sighs, low and private at his ear, the shudder and give of the waves as they reached the shore. Day after day, hour after hour, they kept coming in, whiter than snow or blackthorn blossom, brighter than the sky. It was impossible to believe there could be anything corrupt in them. Where did the dead go to leave such clean water?

Isabella

Orphaned at seventeen, her inheritance a Bible, a blanket, and an ornate comb, Isabella would have been wise to accept John's offer even if she hadn't been watching him from under her lashes for months. They had the banns read on the other side of town and, after an austere wedding (no guests, no feast, only the minister's fee to pay), he brought her to the two-room sandstone cottage he shared with his mother. For the first month, Agnes would not speak to Isabella. Then she would not stop.

A densening tide infiltrated the cells of Isabella's body. She would know where John was by its rise and fall. It became a private joke between them, snatching an embrace as Agnes measured oatmeal or stirred a pot. Isabella would be darning in the last light and John would come to her quietly, kiss her ear, her throat, her breast, his hands searching beneath her clothes. While the older woman slept, muttering, beside the fire, John and Isabella studied the articles of marriage long into the night, provoking sometimes a cry that would jolt Agnes from one dream to another.

Agnes was not used to seeing John smile.

Skinny Isabella, with her blackbird bones, produced child after child. That's enough, Agnes told her, after six. That's more than enough. How will we feed them?

Isabella, with the sated breath of the new baby at her ear, said nothing. This is gold, she thought. This is all the silk and spices anyone could need.

The seventh child fought against coming into the world and broke its mother. Isabella turned whiter and waxier by the day, and then she died.

Agnes would not have the baby put out to nurse. She carried it with her, fed it like an orphan lamb on thin cream sweetened with honey, scalded milk filtered through four layers of muslin. She kept it in her bed, slept and woke with it at night. It had the face of Isabella, the same small eyes and delicate bones. It stared unblinking at Agnes, with something like a frown, as if it could see the unseeable, where Isabella had gone, the lives of its father and grandmother and brothers and sisters unfolding over the years. Agnes sang to it, and it worked its mouth like a mute, flightless bird. The other children, who had never heard Agnes sing, crowded round, sucking at their fingers. Her voice was silty with disuse. She sang hymns and carols and old ballads of faithless lovers. When she forgot the words she substituted whatever came to hand: cup, bannock, mitten, roof, harbour.

No one expected the baby to live, and it did not.

Another James

By happy coincidence, Isabella's death came during a brief upturn in the manufacture of the coarse brown linen for which the town was known, and soon it was employing the whole family. John was a stoker in the boiler room. The girls worked as flax dressers or at the looms. The small children did the jobs to which they were suited, scrambling over the machinery to replace the bobbins and running beneath it to clear the clogging waste. It was not uncommon for the inexperienced to sacrifice digits or limbs or heads to the hundred-foot run, bent double beneath the carriage, and in this way the youngest boy, William, was lost. He lived an hour laid out on the floor of Mr. Doig's office, with his siblings praying over him, but never showed any sign that he heard. The other boys worked their way up to maintaining the looms and other machines. Agnes, with her prematurely bent back and crabbed knuckles, descended through ever more unskilled work, eventually demoted to sweeping up.

As the oldest boy, another James, approached adulthood, his broad face showed furrows of discontent. He looked at the chimneys reaching to the sky, at the processions passing beneath them each morning before the sun rose and each evening after it had set, at his father sitting silent at the end of the day, and he frowned. He looked at the proud, grand buildings gone up in recent decades, three and four storeys, with arches and balustrades and pillars twined with grapevines and palm leaves and monkeys and parrots and elephants, at the new shops with their exotic spoils set out in windows for everyone to see.

On winter evenings after work, he and his brother Thomas went to the night school, where they studied writing, arithmetic, and navigation. This would, it was implied, help the students' children to lead lives free of want, although in every other way very much like their own. He frowned at this, too. The brothers began to argue over trades unions, electoral reform, the proper education of the poor. In these discussions, increasingly heated, Thomas was the more conservative. James seemed to gaze beyond the horizon and see impossible futures. Even the most optimistic of these seemed, to his family, unwelcoming. Change, they suggested, although desirable, should surely stop when it reached its natural conclusion.

James joined a discussion group in which he learned the value of speaking his thoughts in a particular order. He made new friends, men with visions of their own. He became involved in organising Sunday schools at the free church on Mary Street and preached there sometimes. He observed that people outside his family welcomed the opportunity to hear his opinions. He began to talk to his fellow workers about the conditions of their employ. He openly criticised certain practices, some legal and some not, that were common in the factories of the port.

In the next downturn, he and his visionary friends were the first to be turned out, and he could not afterwards find anyone to take him on. He left to seek work elsewhere. A letter came from Bradford, then one from Manchester, where he had found many working men who took the betterment of their lot seriously, as did even some of the manufacturers. Life in that city was hard, he wrote, and dark. He did not see a green thing from one week's end to the next. He missed the clamour of the harbour and the smell of tar and the great flocks of white gulls soaring overhead on long summer evenings and of course his family.

They did not hear from him again. But sometimes, when change and rumours of change rolled into the port, someone would wonder what James might think of this or that proposal, or suggest that, in its expression, a careful listener might detect the inflections of his voice.

Jessie

Jessie was a rectangular girl with a wide smile and bumptious red hair that caused her all manner of bother. She had been teased about it as a child and had become very conscious of its inappropriate energy. At the mill, where the air swirled tawny with lint and fly, her hair was tied up in a handkerchief and had no choice but to do as it was told. But at the end of the day, when she set it free, it seemed to bounce up with renewed vigour, as if it couldn't wait to get out into the world and make trouble. The pennies she had left for herself, after handing the bulk of her wages over to Agnes, were spent on ribbons and hairpins. Sometimes, when Agnes was in a good mood, she would sit Jessie down in front of her and cluck with disapproval as she combed the damp hair into even, flat locks and rolled them up in long strips of brown paper that would transform them overnight to meek and lustrous ringlets.

As Jessie entered her twenties, she had been contributing to the family budget for more than a decade, and while she never for a moment questioned the broad principles of diligence and endurance embodied by her father and grandmother and older siblings, she saw no reason to allow them control over the finer grain of her life. When she started walking out with Alexander McKinnen, she made no effort to hide it, and tossed her head at Agnes and John, who judged him too young and irresponsible. Jessie thought him the handsomest thing she had ever seen. He had dark hair soft as spaniel ears and dark eyes and a delicious, dark voice like the slow morning waves on the beach.

It was a bright, wet spring. The rain fell halfway to earth and then hung in a fine, refractive mist that turned the air white. Under it, the sea shone, too dazzling to look at. The moisture penetrated everything. Jessie and Alexander sheltered under arches and porches and in barns and sheds and once or twice in Alexander's bed when his family was gone. By August, when the sun was blazing and the fields were turning gold, Jessie was beginning to show and Alexander had disappeared, rumoured to have taken a boat for foreign parts.

There had been no promise to break, his family said, no talk of marriage. As for the child, Jessie could appeal to the parish all she liked. No one knew where Alexander was. If the parish wanted to go through his pockets, it was welcome to try to track him down in the wilds of Cape Breton or the cellars of Philadelphia.

The child was born with no will or means to take a breath. Jessie kept to her bed afterwards, and never got strong enough to return to the mill. She died in March, just as spring was starting to brighten the hills once more.

Clementina

After John's death, his remaining children scattered. The girls married and moved away. Thomas took his wife and son to India, leaving only his small daughter behind with Agnes. Clementina was thin and wheezy, prone to coughs and fevers. The Indian climate, everyone agreed, was no place for her. Nor, they added silently, was the Scottish one.

But Clementina kept on living. Knocked down every winter by this illness or that, she got up every spring a little longer and stringier, a stalk of honeysuckle winding up through a thorn bush. She had strong, prominent teeth, like a goat's, and the hair of one accustomed to storms.

Thomas sent money, regularly at first and then not so regularly. There were more children, a new wife, yet more children. News came less often.

Although Clementina was not simple, as some had suggested, she was scatty, easily distracted. She could not be trusted to boil milk or turn a heel. But she was tough and willing and would do whatever work she was given. She laughed often, a big laugh that showed her teeth. (Cover your mouth, Agnes would say, wincing.) She could not remember her mother and showed no interest in the family expanding in India. She brought Agnes violets and seashells and pink stones and sat at her feet crooning nonsense songs in a low voice, more jackdaw than blackbird.

When the mill let Agnes go, she went out charring, took Clementina with her, taught her the limited mysteries of the skivvy. The ladies she worked for—Mrs. Doig, Mrs. Finlay, Widow Reid—would not look Clementina in the eye but made no objection to her scrubbing their floors.

In the year of Agnes's eighty-ninth birthday, Thomas's second wife took to her bed, and he sent for Clementina. It was time for his daughter to take up her duties, keep house, look after the little ones.

No, said Clementina.

She felt nothing for Thomas or her older brother. She couldn't recall the names or even the number of the other children. India she thought of as a faerie land of scarlet trees, bejewelled frogs, holy men puffing at intricately carved pipes, lions and tigers and giraffes ambling through the streets and pushing their heads into people's kitchens. (Although in the photographs Thomas had sent, studio portraits of the family smartly dressed and holding one another's shoulders as if to form a fence, it resembled nothing more than Mrs. Doig's elegant morning room.) Clementina imagined Thomas's wife (her stepmother, Agnes reminded her) as something like Mrs. Doig must have been when younger—quick and sharp and pale and always trying to catch people out.

Thomas had paid for her passage. But he couldn't put her on the steamer.

Agnes explained what an opportunity this was for a girl like her. Although yes, undeniably, in a frightening, alien land. How Clementina would have brothers and sisters for the first time. Albeit strangers. How well Thomas was doing—the manager of a jute mill—and how comfortable her new home would be. Even if it was in a town of foreigners. The family had, Agnes added in a hushed tone uncommitted to admiration or disdain, a servant. (Also foreign.)

What is he like? Clementina asked, meaning her father.

Agnes tried to remember. He was tall, she thought. Was that right, or was he the shorter one? He was quiet and patient, she seemed to recall. He had a little dog once. He named it Tip and taught it to sit on its hind legs and take scraps from his hand.

Clementina considered this. I would like a dog, she said.

Conversations, Agnes found, were longer and more convoluted than they used to be. She found herself always lagging a step or two behind.

I would call him Stanley, Clementina said.

If they even have dogs in India, Agnes said.

Would you miss me? Clementina asked. If I were to go?

Agnes

Agnes seemed to need less and less sleep. There was a small window next to the bed she had shared with Clementina, and she would lie awake listening to the wind and the rain and the mice in the walls and the noise of the sea that never stopped.

People said it was like breathing, but Agnes heard no ebb and flow. It was constant, a sigh that went on forever.

When she did finally doze, she felt a temporary ease, as if the fossilised debris lodged in her joints had been replaced by a kindly, elastic element. As if she could kneel without pain, walk without pain. As if she could swim or dance or do whatever she wished.

And then her old dream would return again, the dream of a tide that never fell but only kept rising, over the harbour, over the boatyards and mills of the foreshore, over the shops and churches and grand buildings of the town. And still on it came, surging up the hill, flooding through the streets, encircling the house, lapping at the walls. It rose all the way to the upper window, and slid into the room, cool as the moon and dark as the starless sky.

This time, she said, although there was no one to hear her, it is not a dream.

For a moment, the tide paused, just long enough for her to snatch up a blue ribbon she had once been given, and an old peg doll dressed in salvaged scraps of cloth, then it lifted her in its hundred soft hands and carried her on.

The Ground the Deck

W HEN Megan first moved to London, she lived in the top of a house at the top of Brixton Hill that seemed to her, all fresh and green and hopeful as she was, the very best place in the city. She had been staying in a thieves' hostel near Victoria while she was looking for somewhere to live, eating biscuits and sleeping in her clothes, and the first six flat shares she'd been to see didn't want her, so she was grateful beyond words when Licia and Xander said they'd love to have her live with them, they were kindred spirits, she could move in just as soon as she liked, that very day if she wanted.

Right now in fact, Licia said. Go and fetch your things. I cannot *bear* another minute cooped up here with no one but Xander.

Xander inclined his head slowly towards Megan. I am inured to her insults, he said.

Megan thought of the Underground, in which she had got lost twice already, and the two lumpy unmanageable body bags that held everything she had imagined she would need in the world. It might take me a couple of trips, she said.

Xander will go with you, Licia said.

Because I have nothing better to do than run around at her whim, said Xander.

It'll be good for him. He hasn't opened the front door in days.

I'll have you know, darling—

But Licia interrupted him. You should get a taxi.

A taxi, Megan said. How much would that cost?

In fact, let's all go. It'll be fun.

And that was what they did. They took the Tube to Victoria and Megan repacked the few items she had dared to unpack while Licia and Xander waited, scrutinising the narrow bed and the sticky floor but paying no attention to the NO SMOKING signs. Downstairs, at some invisible, practised gesture from Licia, a taxi appeared, and they rode through the snarled traffic at a processional crawl, as if to allow their subjects the opportunity to wave.

*

The flat was in a red-brick terrace near the prison and was perfectly adequate for two people, which was the number on the lease. With three squeezed in, it became almost affordable, but only by caring for money more than it deserved. If Megan had been stopped in the street at this time and quizzed on the subject, she could have told the name and age of every coin in her purse. But this was just a rough patch, she knew. They would beat through it to the lives they were supposed to live, where they would subsist on air and art and sunlight.

Licia was working in a gallery, a position too sought after to require adequate payment, and taking classes in life drawing and photography and printmaking until she could decide in which medium exactly her talents lay. The flat would often be obstructed for days by some piece that was struggling to meet her standards. Megan had one of her half-finished oils in her room, a woman looking out suspiciously, or perhaps eagerly, from a patch of murky blue. She had told Licia she liked it as it was. Take it, Licia said. It's hideous. It's doomed. I never want to see it again.

Xander was signing on and working at what he always referred to as his first novel. He admired writers like Lowry and Hemingway, who drank enormous amounts and produced their novels effortlessly in their sleep, and was doing his best to emulate them. The novel was forever stopping and starting, the plot reversing, the characters changing age and century and gender. But any day now, they were all confident, it would come flowing out, fully formed.

Megan had found a temporary data-entry job because she could type very fast and people would pay you to do that, although not quite enough to live on. What she wanted to do was work in television or film or magazines, something with a clear story told in pictures. Her idea of what this would entail was hazy. She saw herself progressing to a position of authority where the pictures would be at her disposal, together with minions, who at a flick of her finger would proffer the day's options. She pursued this vision of her future mainly by sending out begging letters. Dear Sir or Madam, Please employ me. I have German and Art History, I can ride a unicycle and once organised a charity fashion show, I am full of talent and creativity, ask anyone. Occasionally, they would write back to express regret or pity, which she took as proof that her strategy would succeed. In the meantime, she got up cruelly early every day to take a bus and two Tubes so that she could spend seven and a half hours keying in requisition orders for the multitude of small and large pieces on which a railway depends for its continued smooth running.

The downstairs flat had the garden and their flat had the balcony overlooking the garden. All winter it meant nothing to them. They put a blanket over the window to keep the heat in; they might as well have lived in a cave. But as soon as the weather turned warm, they took the blanket down and opened the window wide. There was just enough room on the balcony for three kitchen chairs, and they would sit in a row, their knees pressed against the railings, looking out over the top of the prison and the backs of houses, the gardens and sheds and blocks of flats stretching down the hill to where the riots had been. Licia and Xander liked to imagine what they would do if there were riots again, how they would listen to the sirens, watch the fires burn, the smoke hanging in the sky like a dirty fog. But there were no riots, and no wars either. Or if there were wars, they were so contained and far away it was hard to be sure if they were wars or something else. There was no blackout, no rationing, no conscription. No one required them to participate or even protest. Gradually, the colours would fade and lights would start to come on here and there. The air smelled of petrol and dust, that small London dust that was invisible and sharp as glass and forever insinuating its way into clothes. There would be traffic noise from the hill, and fragments of conversation from the road in front, and always a blackbird sobbing out its song from the heart of a lilac. As the evening cooled, they would fetch the blanket that had hung over the window and settle it around their knees. The buildings and gardens would sink into a pool of darkness that deepened and spread as the streetlamps glowed brighter, and they would look out over it all, like passengers on an ocean liner, watching over the bow rails as the dreaming blue land of their future rose on the horizon, hurrying nearer with every moment, its lights winking hope and promise.

*

But that was later. First there was the winter to get through and the winding alleys of new acquaintance to be charted.

A few weeks after Megan moved in, Licia took her to lunch with an elderly aunt and uncle. Megan was invited, she supposed, only because Xander was engaged elsewhere, although what excuse would have withstood the force of Licia's will she couldn't imagine. Before they went into the restaurant, Licia listed suitable and unsuitable topics of conversation for her. The waiters spoke in French, and everyone except Megan replied in French. The aunt and uncle told stories about palaces in Venice and villas in Paris, penthouse apartments overlooking Central Park where a new pane of glass had to be winched up the side of the building, inch by inch. With no home of their own, they toured from one of these places to the next, staying for weeks, months, in spacious chambers where an extra guest or two would hardly show. Aunt Bea had a calm round face, untouched by the age that had crumpled her body, and seemed to Megan at peace with the world.

Afterwards, Licia exclaimed at Megan's naivety. She's the most frightful snob, Licia said. And she bosses Uncle Teddy around, you have no idea.

Really?

She was dirt poor before she met him. I mean *dirt* poor. And since she got hold of the purse strings, she hasn't allowed him the least say. Not the *least*.

Licia herself did not believe in restricting her lifestyle to her earnings, and was in the happy position of not having to. Her parents (The Parents, she called them, as if they were the only ones in the world) were forever buying her extravagant gifts and sending her hampers from Fortnum and Mason. Every spring and autumn, she and her mother went out to buy Licia a new summer wardrobe and a new winter wardrobe. If Licia were to peer from the top of a tall staircase, or teeter along a perilous rooftop, she would see The Parents waiting below, with mattresses spread out to catch her, duvets and goosedown pillows. The feathers buoyed her steps; her feet, in their Italian leather shoes, never quite made contact with the pavement. She was always the one turning up the heat or throwing out two-day-old bread or buying white rum and vermouth to make cocktails.

Xander came from a rich family too, but he had fallen out with them, possibly over the writer thing, or maybe the gay thing; anyway, he didn't see them at all, except sometimes an aspiring-politician brother he despised. Oh darling, he said when Megan asked him about the brother. He's exactly the kind of truffle-grubbing breeder you would expect. And so is his wife and that dreadful piglet child.

Xander considered himself independent, and was proud of it. His only responsibility was to go down to the dole office every Wednesday to confirm that he was alive and actively looking for work. He answered these questions without embarrassment, and probably they heard his answers without surprise. It was enough finding jobs for the yearning masses who came in every day banging their fists on the counter and weeping, without having to worry about Xander. Every so often, for the sake of form perhaps, they sent him on an interview. He made not the slightest effort to appear anything other than he was—turning up in his red silk slash-front shirt with his hair tumbling across his eyes, folding his long limbs into martyred poses, calling the interviewer darling—and no one had yet shown any interest in employing him in even the most menial position.

As for Megan, she didn't have much family, and what there was had nothing of anything at all. She had never known her father, a sailor who'd come ashore just long enough to whirl her mother round the Palais and leave her with the name of his ship on the back of a cigarette packet. Years later, when Megan tried to track him down, she found out it was not, in fact, a ship, but a signalling base in the middle of the country. The Navy, she discovered, names all its establishments as if they are ships, and acts as if they are at sea, so her father would have said port and starboard, and taken shore leave, and called the ground the deck, even if he never felt it roll beneath him.

Megan's grandparents threw her mother out when they learned she was pregnant. But a couple of years later, when Megan's grandmother died, Grandad Charlie relented and let her move back in. Mostly so that she could take care of him and Megan's Auntie Dot, who couldn't read or write, and needed a lot of taking care of.

Shortly before Megan moved to London, Grandad Charlie died unexpectedly, and there was no money to pay for the funeral. Charlie might have been an old curmudgeon who hadn't been very kind to Megan's mother or her grandmother, or to anyone actually, but he still needed, deserved even, a send-off. Megan's mother was so distressed by it she became altogether helpless. I don't know what to do, she kept saying. What will people think? Auntie Dot came to the rescue, for surely the first and only time in her life, by remembering Harry the Insurance Man. Harry used to come round every Friday when Megan was small, collecting the mite that people set aside for death and disaster. He often used to stop and have a cup of tea with them. They were his favourite customers, he always said. How are my favourite customers today? The insurance company didn't know anything about Harry. They were interested only in the papers that Grandad Charlie, who'd got paranoid in his last years, had shredded or burned or eaten. Megan spent two whole days on the phone, and finally they paid up. It was nothing, the merest pittance, but it did buy a coffin and enough flowers piled on top of it to let her mother look the neighbours in the eye.

Megan swore that she was never going to find herself in that situation again. A few weeks later, she got on a coach and waved goodbye to her mother and Auntie Dot. Through the salt-grimed windows, they were already hard to distinguish from the other aunts and mothers, leaning in the cold, hugging their coats tight. She smiled at them and let herself believe that they were smiling back. She knew she was doing the right thing. She was going to a place where nobody sat waiting for death and disaster, a place where people lived rich cultural lives, went to the opera and the ballet and the theatre, discussed the important matters of the day, and, when the walls of inequality and injustice towered too high, got together to break them down.

She did not, of course, expect all this to be laid at her feet the moment she arrived.

Every day that winter, she got up in the dark and pulled on socks and coat to go to the bathroom, often passing a sleeping Xander on the way. Megan's name was not on the lease, but because she was paying rent, she had her own room, while Xander usually shared with Licia. But Licia would bring home some studded youth she'd found in the street, or she and Xander would squabble, and then Xander would end up on the couch, bundled up in the icy predawn, perfectly still, like one of those bundles Megan would see an hour later when she came up out of the Tube, a bundle of clothes in a doorway, wrapped so tight it was hard to tell which end was which or whether the person inside was alive or dead, and she would count her blessings, burrowing her face down into her coat, although less than a minute later she would forget she was blessed, as she pushed through biting wind and crowds to reach an old-fashioned office block where a middle-aged woman called Eunice, who wore a wig and dressed like the Queen, had power of life and death over Megan and the other data-entry staff.

Megan was very good at this monotonous, ridiculous job. She raced through her requisition forms with hardly an error. Because of this, Eunice, who was a tyrant—returning work arbitrarily, indulging her favourites and bullying everyone else—started to show her a grudging respect. I will say this, she said, looking over her glasses as if she'd spotted a talking monkey, you are careful in your work (rolling the word careful over several syllables in her St. Kitts accent). Once or twice there was a condolence letter to do, when an employee had been killed on the railway, and Eunice assigned these to Megan. She felt a touch of pride in this small distinction, although she felt nothing at all about the man who had died or the widow she was writing to.

At the end of the day, she pushed back down into the Underground, shuffled on to a train. At Brixton, the crowds battled to get out of the station. There would be policemen at the entrance, trying to look cheerful and approachable, the riots were in the past, everyone was on the same side now. But the younger ones were jumpy, touching their conspicuous hats for reassurance as the currents surged around them. Outside, the queues for the bus were ten thick, people shoved and wrestled, knocked one another to the floor. Megan would pick herself up, brush herself off, wait for the next bus.

What she dreamed of, what she craved, on the bus, on the Tube, standing in queues for the bus and the Tube, was sleep.

She had used to imagine that if she had a lot of money, she would buy art and a space to hang it, vast windows through which light would pour to reveal truth and beauty. Now it seemed to her what anyone would buy was sleep. That would be the first thing. After that, food and clothes and swimming pools. Then you'd put a big lilo in your swimming pool and sleep there too.

On the weekend, she wouldn't move until eleven or twelve or whatever time Licia's latest went out the door and Licia came past her room crying, What was I thinking? Whatever was I thinking? Which was what she said about all of them except for that brief period when she'd been in love with Benjamin the alcoholic architect. But that had ended badly. When Megan went through, Xander would be sitting on the couch, his duvet wrapped around him and a little cloud of smoke above his head. They'd make tea and toast, turn on the radio, and sit there in their cave. After a while, Megan would fetch the paper from the hall and they would go through it picking out jobs for which she was totally unqualified. You have to start at the top, Licia would say, when Megan protested.

She didn't go to the opera or the ballet or the theatre, because she couldn't afford it. She went sometimes to museums, those that were free, and to openings at Licia's gallery, which were also free and where there was wine. Occasionally, they went down to the Ritzy or the Academy, or up to the South Bank or Camden. But mostly they just hung out, dissecting Licia's young men, mocking people they worked with, or laughing about Licia's mother's charity lunches, Xander's father's model soldiers, everything they had escaped.

And so in this way the winter passed, long months of it, each one much the same as the last. Xander had rewritten the first page of his novel thirty times. Licia had abandoned equal numbers of men and works of art. And Megan was still, for the moment, ordering parts at the railway.

*

Towards the end of that winter, three things happened that seemed to Megan later to have been related with a significance she didn't note at the time.

Firstly, she was offered a job, not the job she had applied for but a more lowly position. Much more lowly, an assistant to the assistant absolute nobody, as Licia said. The salary was less even than Megan was making at the railway. And look, said Licia, it's not even in London. You'd have to move out to some frightful soulless suburb. You don't want to leave us, do you? After much agonising, Megan decided not to accept it. There would be other, better jobs, as Licia said. The very thing you wanted, in Licia's experience, always came along sooner or later.

Secondly, new tenants moved into the downstairs flat. They seemed too young to be married, barely schoolchildren, but that's what it said on their post, Mr. and Mrs. Unwin, Mrs. C Unwin. They both worked for the Inland Revenue, Xander reported, or some other dull and unsavoury branch of the civil service. They were small and frail, and clung to each other when they walked down the street, like refugees in a storm.

Notes began to appear, slid under the door of the flat early in the morning or late at night. To Our Upstairs Neighbours, they began, and were signed Your Downstairs Neighbours. In between, there would be a reasonably worded plea for the better management of their shared space. Pick the post up off the hall floor. Don't overfill the bins. Then a cheerleading exclamation mark. Better for us all! We hope you agree!

In all the years Licia and Xander had been in the flat they had hardly registered that people lived downstairs. Can you believe their cheek? they said. Who are they anyway? They made fun of the Unwins' cheap clothes and regular hours, as if poverty and a steady job were peculiar new concepts. They piled the bins higher, left the milk bottles rolling in the path, walked right over the post. The unseen hands of the Unwins continued to make their appeals. The exclamation marks doubled, tripled. Then the notes stopped. The Unwins receded into the shadows beyond the hall, where nobody was required to think of them.

The third thing was that Xander fell madly, utterly, over-whelmingly in love with a playwright/plasterer he met in the dole queue, and disappeared for several weeks. In his absence, Licia took Megan to some private views. She put her arm through Megan's and introduced her to sleek, bright bird-people as My good friend, Megan. They cooked dinner together, pasta or baked potatoes. They curled up on the couch, and Licia told Megan how much she envied her hair and what she should do with it. She pointed out how her own hair had been cut to divert attention from her worst features (she particularly disliked her nose), a style it had taken most of her life and an outrageously expensive hairdresser to discover and to which she would now be faithful. They sat up late drinking Licia's vodka until they were full of hope and nostalgia. Megan told Licia about her hazy dreams, the pictures and the minions. She told her about her mother and her Auntie Dot and the mistake (Megan) that had set the course of her mother's life. If either of them got ill or died, she would have to go back, so she'd always thought at least, to look after the other one. (Madness! said Licia. Suicide!) She told Licia about her sailor father, roving, as she then believed, across the steep rolling seas. Which was not something she told everybody. Licia told Megan about every boyfriend she'd had since the age of twelve, every one of them a fool and not one able to make her believe for a moment that she was any better than she was. This was, she said, why she had liked Benjamin the alcoholic architect, who was straight-talking and had never tried to flatter her. He had seen through her from the start, and for this reason she had felt safe with him. Although, as it turned out, she had not been.

When Xander returned, forlorn and rejected and minus his meagre savings, which he had either spent on or given to the plasterer/playwright in a fruitless attempt to retain his affections, Licia gathered him in and set about comforting him, exactly as, it turned out, she had done all the other times this had happened. Suddenly, Licia and Xander were whispering in corners, exchanging meaningful looks, changing the subject when Megan entered the room. Xander looked thinner than ever, his hair drooped, his eyes were red and bruised. But in Megan's hearing, anything he said about the affair was upbeat, ironic. Licia, in Megan's hearing, never mentioned it.

Gradually, Xander returned to his old self. His hair regained its bounce, he and Licia began bickering again, and the three of them went back to hanging out together. By then the season had changed.

*

There was no spring that year. No scent of cut grass, no blossom, no softening breeze flicking playfully at knees and curtains. All at once it was hot and oppressive. The leaves on the trees blackened and dropped. The flowers withered. Even the weeds that chanced their luck in the cracks between pavement and houses shrivelled. In the park near the flat, there was nothing but dust and gravel. The children flung themselves down on the gravel and cried, the teenagers threw cigarettes, the lovers quarrelled, the dogs fought.

Their small balcony was a gateway cut into the dome of heat. They passed through it into the evening air, looking out in pity at the rest of London lying flat and defeated below them. They drank muddy brown cocktails improvised with Licia's blender and fruit sold off cheap at the market, and congratulated themselves on their wisdom.

We could be making car parts, said Licia. Or selling ad space.

Or working in the plastic-bucket factory, said Megan, who had done this for a month one summer.

Or worse, drawled Xander. We could be in stocks and shares.

Licia frowned at Xander. Anyway, she said. We're very wise.

Although actually, said Megan, I hate my job.

You'll find something, said Licia. I mean how long have you been here? No time at *all!*

I suppose so, said Megan. Although that was less true this week than it had been last. She had had to borrow this month's rent from Licia. And on the inside of her smart—her only—jacket, she had found a hard, flaking grey spot where some person on the bus had, for who knows what reason, quietly reached inside and pressed their chewing gum into the lining.

Then Licia surprised Megan by asking what she wanted to do for her birthday in a week's time.

I'm going home.

No no *no!* said Licia. It's your first birthday with us.

They'll have made a cake.

We can make a cake.

Xander rolled his eyes. We can buy a cake, he said.

Megan knew her mother would have already got her a present, a blouse, say, that she would have saved up for and that Megan would never wear, and she would have helped Auntie Dot buy some trinket, and written a card for her. They would watch her unwrap these presents and her mother would say, Is it all right, hen? You can take it back if you want. Are you sure it's all right? I kept the receipt. And then they would ask about her job, which they considered a miracle of loaves and fishes, neither of them having the faintest idea how anybody went about getting a job. It would be warm in the flat, but they wouldn't open the windows. They had a horror of catching a chill.

You absolutely *must* stay here, said Licia. And you must have a party.

I don't know anyone to have a party for.

Of course you do. There's that cousin of yours, Yvette.

Yvette was some kind of step-relation whose details Megan's mother had insisted on copying out when Megan moved to London. They had met up a couple of times early on. Yvette wore wide print skirts and what looked like pearls. She was proud that she had mostly lost her accent, and asked Megan how long she would keep hers. She talked a lot about her work, which Megan was given to understand was very demanding, and particularly about her boss, how he joked about seeing more of Yvette than his wife, how he was building a dovecot in his garden for his daughter's wedding.

I don't think so, said Megan.

Then there's Isaac, Licia continued.

Xander made a noise that indicated derision.

Megan had met Isaac at Licia's gallery. She had been struck by his eyes and the large hole in his jumper, which she took to be daring rather than slovenly, and how he studied each picture at length before forming an implacable judgement. Isaac was a poet and held strong opinions on a range of subjects. He particularly admired Henry Miller and carried *Tropic of Cancer* like a large medal pinned to his chest. Licia and Xander sniggered at him and made fun of his poetry, so Megan stopped taking him to the flat. Instead, they went to his bedsit in Vauxhall, where there was one glass and one plate and he recited passages out of books she had failed to read, and criticised her underwear.

I don't actually see him any more, she said.

And I'll invite those people from downstairs, said Licia.

Xander groaned. Oh, darling, no. They're such hicks. I swear they must be Appalachian.

Appalachian pinheads, said Licia.

They're probably brother and sister, said Xander.

Incestuous Appalachian pinheads.

Xander and Licia could keep this up for some time. Even if I were having a party, Megan said, I wouldn't invite them.

And there's my college friends, said Licia. I can bring a whole crowd.

Licia's college friends were freakishly tall and wore sparkly clothes and told the same anecdotes over and over.

Nor them, Megan said.

Xander leaned towards Megan as if to whisper, but he didn't whisper. You know why she wants a party? he said. She wants to invite her new man.

What new man?

Her mother introduced them. He has a house in Chelsea and a Jag. Ask her what he does.

Xander knows perfectly well what he does, said Licia.

She's afraid to say it aloud.

He works in the City.

He's a stockbroker! said Xander.

They despised stockbrokers. Also bankers, lawyers, estate agents. Anyone who made money.

Si's passionate about art, said Licia. He bought a painting from me.

He's not *passionate*, darling. He invests in it. It's all gilt-edged bonds to him.

Xander's jealous, said Licia. Si's charming. And witty. And there's absolutely nothing wrong with having a house in Chelsea.

So will we be meeting him? Xander persisted.

Anyway, you don't know him, said Licia. It would be a little odd for you to invite him to your party.

I'm not having a party, Megan reminded her.

She finally managed to persuade Licia that there would be no party. But she did agree to stay and spend her birthday with Licia and Xander. Your best friends, as Licia said. Licia would cook dinner (Xander rolled his eyes again) and they would have a fabulous time.

*

Licia told Megan dinner would be at eight and she was not to come any earlier. After work, she walked round a park near the office. It was hotter than ever and she could feel the ruts in the path through her impractical thin sandals. She went to a museum that was open late. She was the only person there, slapping through corridors of pouty dukes and duchesses like some stranded sea creature.

On the way to the Tube she rang home. Did you get the parcel? her mother asked immediately. She had never trusted the post office, or anything else that claimed to traverse the country purposefully to arrive at a known destination. I still have the receipt, she said. Then, as an afterthought, Happy birthday. She asked how Megan was spending her day, and Megan said she'd been at work. Really? her mother said. That's wonderful. Megan said Licia was going to bake a cake, and her mother said, Really, hen? Well, that's wonderful. Then she put Auntie Dot on and Megan had to go through it again, the post, work, the cake.

As she approached the flat, she could hear noise, and she knew, sinkingly, what it would be. She realised she had known all along.

All the people she'd said she didn't want to see were there. Yvette, Isaac, the Unwins. Also seven or eight of Licia's tallest and sparkliest friends, a junkie friend of Xander's who'd once told Megan she had the hands of a washerwoman, and Benjamin the alcoholic architect, whose name she had been forbidden to mention on pain of death.

Licia came hurrying up. Meggy Peg, you're here. Happy birthday. Isn't this fabulous?

We said dinner.

But this is better. Come and have a drink.

She let Licia pour her wine and tell her what fun it was and pour more wine and tell her how she'd happened to bump into Benjamin and pour more wine until slowly gravity started to lose its hold. Xander drifted over and wished Megan happy birthday and hissed in Licia's ear before drifting away. They must be quarrelling again. Megan started to think how nice it was of Licia to do this, even though she had promised not to, and what a good friend she was, the best friend, possibly, that she had ever had. She told her this, several times, and Licia agreed. Megan looked around at all the people she didn't want to see and found she couldn't focus on them anyway.

Some of Licia's friends were dancing. In their shimmery short dresses and bare legs they swayed dreamily, underwater flowers on long stalks. The rest of Licia's friends and Isaac were lined up on the couch watching in silence, as if it were a show they had sneaked into without paying.

Everyone's so dressed up, Megan said. She was wearing a skirt she'd bought from Oxfam her last year in school.

You look great, said Licia, not looking. Now you must mingle. And listen, if you speak to Benjamin, do tell him how pleased you are that he's here.

Megan watched the dancers, swaying a little herself. Mingle, she repeated. After a while Benjamin came over, looking for wine. He felt about for the corkscrew. Megan handed it to him and he looked at her as if she had been deliberately concealing it.

I remember you, he said. Licia's friend.

I remember you too, she said. Licia's . . . Benjamin.

So, it's your birthday, he said. According to the invite.

It occurred to Megan that Xander had been wrong. Licia hadn't wanted to have this party so that she could ask Si, she had wanted to have it so that she could ask Benjamin.

He asked her what she was doing now, and she told him about the requisition forms.

You're still doing that? He stared at her. Really?

Just for now, she said. It's temporary.

Yesterday, Eunice had handed her an application form for a job on the next floor. You should apply for this, Eunice had said. It's more money.

It was a lot more money. It wouldn't hurt, Megan had thought, to be making more money while she was waiting for the very thing she wanted to come along.

How long has it been? Benjamin said.

It's not so different from Licia working in the gallery, she said.

Ah, but Licia, he said. It doesn't matter what Licia does. She's just going to get married to some rich guy and spend her days chatting up Tory wives while he screws the country.

Was he really an alcoholic, she tried to remember, or was that just one of those things Licia said?

You can't do things to order, she said. This had made perfect sense in her head. It's not like making cakes. That is, plastic buckets.

Don't get sucked in, he said.

I don't know what you mean.

When I get up in the morning, I have to work. Otherwise, I starve. It's a wonderful discipline.

I should mingle, Megan said.

What did he know anyway? If his life was so great, how come he was an alcoholic?

She manoeuvred around the dancers. The junkie gave her an evil look, so she steered around him too and found herself face to face with the Unwins.

Hi, Megan said.

They looked at her as if they expected her to add some witty repartee.

It's my birthday.

We knew it was somebody's birthday, said Mrs. Unwin.

Megan remembered the bins suddenly. She hoped they wouldn't start on that.

Are you the one who goes out early? Mrs. Unwin said.

I suppose I am. She had never been this close to the Unwins before. Mrs. Unwin was small and dark and pointy, Mr. Unwin was mousy and pale. Not much sibling resemblance.

And then there's the one who comes in late, Mrs. Unwin said. And the one who hardly goes out at all. The writer.

You do know a lot about us.

Oh yes. Mrs. Unwin seemed to think Megan had said something funny. Out on that balcony. We hear everything.

They had been right underneath all along. How odd that she had never thought of that. In her imagination they took their soft bodies into their flat and shut the door and ceased to exist.

It's been quite an education, said Mrs. Unwin.

Oh dear, said Megan.

Mrs. Unwin laughed again, touched her arm. Don't worry, we're only teasing.

At least you don't steal our mail, Mr. Unwin said.

They both laughed loudly at this.

Of course, Neil works at home so much, Mrs. Unwin said.

He does? Neil must be Mr. Unwin. Who worked at the Inland Revenue.

Yes. His book. Virgil.

You're doing a book on Virgil? Megan stared at him. For the Inland Revenue?

They both looked at her, and laughed again.

Perhaps it was another branch of the civil service after all. I should mingle, she said.

Some time later, she found herself at the front door. She congratulated herself for having circumnavigated the room. The next thing must be to turn around and go back.

Xander was out on the balcony. His whole manner told Megan that he was sulking. He was holding a box of chocolates (her birthday chocolates!) and was engaged in taking a bite from each one, and throwing the discarded halves over the balcony. Nearby, Yvette was talking to the junkie. Megan wondered what he would say about *her* hands. Licia's friends were still dancing, arms drifting in the current. Licia was dancing now too, not with but in front of Benjamin. She swayed and sparkled and was in that light barely distinguishable from the other dancers. Benjamin watched her. Megan wondered if he knew about the house in Chelsea.

She found herself in the kitchen and saw her cake. From somewhere grand by the look of it, Harrods or Fortnum. Licia could have put it on The Parents' account. Megan had a vision of her mother's cake, with piped decorations, which she was good at, and candles. She shivered. Perhaps she had caught a chill from the open window. That's funny, she said aloud, and started eating cake.

When she came out, the music had slowed and the room was pitching and rolling in time with it. Air, Megan thought, and headed for the window. She started to hear raised voices.

Xander was still out on the balcony, and the voices were his and Mrs. Unwin's.

Extraordinarily inconsiderate, Mrs. Unwin was saying.

Xander was staring at her silently. He could get vicious when drunk. More than once Megan had seen Licia pull him out of a bar before someone hit him.

Unacceptable, said Mrs. Unwin.

People started to turn. Licia, seeing Xander in trouble, abandoned Benjamin and moved towards the balcony.

Throwing your rubbish into our garden, Mrs. Unwin went on. Wrappers. Apple cores. Bottles even.

Megan felt all of a sudden sober. She remembered tossing apple cores at the back fence. And an evening where they had sat spitting cherry stones over the balcony, competitively. They hadn't given the Unwins a thought. It was as if they had really believed that their physical elevation, arrived at by an accident of small ads and tenancy dates, gave them the right to drop things on those who, by similar accident, lived on the ground.

At that moment someone stopped the music.

You are a peasant, said Xander in the sudden silence. You have a soul of mud. You should go back down the mine so we don't have to see your peasant face.

Mrs. Unwin did not weep or swoon, Mr. Unwin did not shout or raise his fists. They both looked at Xander as if they were memorising his features, and then Mrs. Unwin said, You are very drunk. We can discuss this tomorrow. And she turned round and so did Mr. Unwin and they headed towards the door.

I'll still be drunk tomorrow, Xander said to their backs. No, I mean, I'll be sober and you'll still be—

But they had gone.

The party broke up quickly after that. The music stayed off. People hugged Licia and thanked her, as if the party had been for her. Xander stayed leaning at the balcony, motionless except for his eyes, which kept sliding down and then twitching up, as if repeatedly surprised.

I feel so bad, said Megan, when Licia rejoined them.

What a calf, said Xander. Such a fuss.

But she's right, said Megan. I don't know what we've been thinking.

You would say that.

What do you mean?

He inclined his head slowly towards her. All peasants together.

Xander! Licia said. But she laughed.

Megan looked at her.

Licia shrugged. He took something earlier, she said. He's off his head.

My mind is perfectly clear, said Xander. Then he slid down the window frame and sat down hard and closed his eyes. Perfectly clear.

He may have stayed there all night. Licia turned her attention back to Benjamin and Megan took a bottle of wine to bed with her.

*

A week later it started raining. It soaked through the dust. It flooded along the gutters. It washed the withered leaves out of their corners, pushed them along the pavements, banked them up under walls and railings. All over the city, tidelines appeared, as if the sea had come through in the night.

Licia and Megan sat watching the rain pouring down the windows and collecting on the balcony. Megan told Licia how she used to imagine raindrops were conquering hordes, each new line of rain wiping out the line in front of it, and Licia told Megan she was moving into the house in Chelsea and Xander was going back to his parents.

What? Megan said.

His father's going to sponsor him. Let him finish his novel. So long as he lives at home.

Megan wondered how this could have happened when Xander hadn't talked to his father in years.

Si and I are going to choose the ring this week, Licia went on.

Megan thought of the money she'd borrowed from Licia and wondered how she would pay it back. Neither a borrower nor a lender be, her mother used to say. She wondered where she would live now. She thought of the hostel and how she used to put her purse under her pillow at night.

I'm sorry, Meggy Peg. You'll forgive us, won't you?

Is this what you and Xander have been arguing about?

You've got time to find somewhere else, Licia said. We've got this place until the end of the month.

You don't even fancy him. Megan had finally met Si a few days before, and it was noticeable that Licia kept twitching him off, absently, like a circling fly.

I can help you look if you like.

A stockbroker!

We'll still be best friends, Licia said. You and me. Kindred spirits. Nothing will ever change that.

*

These are the things Megan did that week. She took out the application form that had been folded in the bottom of her bag since Eunice gave it to her and threw it away. She bought an *Evening Standard* and circled some flat shares. She circled some job adverts too. Assistants to assistants to assistants. She took her jacket to the dry cleaners to have the gum removed. She spent the last of the money she didn't have on a pair of shoes that would stand the weather. She tied her hair back and studied her reflection and saw that she was the same as she had been. Then in her salvaged jacket and her waterproof shoes, she set out into the rain.

The Invisible

Across the lake

M R. Ingram and his Invisible daughter Miss Ingram live close by, Martha tells us, in a grand, impractical mansion of the type the wealthy favour—except Invisible, of course—made from dressed stone the colour of spring cream, with a slate roof and glass in every window.

Is that so? we say.

They receive numerous Invisible guests, Martha tells us, who must travel here from other Invisible mansions, in other parts of the country.

That would follow, we say.

They attend fairs and sales about the district. They are regulars at our Wednesday markets.

To sell or to buy?

They are Invisible!

To accomplish trade both parties must be visible, a fact we have not previously had cause to contemplate.

Mr. Ingram's mansion, Martha tells us, stands on the other side of the lake, at the foot of the mountain. We have inspected the spot she indicates and confirmed it is in no way remarkable. Cold eels of water slide among rushes and sedges and tumps of starry moss. Cat-gorse and furze cling to rafts of drier ground. Spearwort and flag dip their toes and shiver.

Not that we need to search for evidence. If there were a mansion across the lake, our dogs would be howling every time an Ingram passed by. Our daughters would be scouring their pots, our sons sweating in their stables and gardens.

Some accuse Martha of fraud, although what she has to gain by it we cannot determine.

Others say her wits are failing. We've known her to put her clothes on back to front and summon her cow with the call meant for hogs. She will stop for minutes on end to watch rooks or lapwings tumble about the sky, as if they bore porridge and dates and the answers to life's mysteries in their beaks.

But most are happy, eager even, to take her at her word. We want to believe that the Invisible have, for whatever purpose, established their Invisible home next to us. It pleases us to imagine them prodding the fat rumps of our livestock, testing our grain with their clean Invisible fingernails.

Tell us more, we say, and Martha dimples like a girl.

There are many of them, she says. Sometimes the Invisible outnumber other visitors.

But why do they come to market?

For amusement, I suppose. Entertainment.

We look each other up and down, wondering which of us is most entertaining.

The Ingrams have called at Martha's cottage, of an evening, to pay their respects.

Miss Ingram has such pale hands, Martha says. As if she keeps them folded away in a linen chest.

What language do they speak?

It is English, I presume. I seem to understand some of it. But their speech is strange. Until you are very close, it's like a noise of leaves or water.

We cannot think why, of all of us, they would choose Martha. She is not the most educated or wise. Not even the most gullible.

Invite us along next time they visit, says Jacob. That should sort the wheat from the goats.

They wouldn't allow it, Martha says.

What are you afraid of? Jacob says. Let's settle this once and for all.

Come on, Martha, we say. Let's settle this. Unless you have reason to be afraid.

I would love to see Miss Ingram's dress, says Eliza. And her jewellery. I would love to see how she does her hair.

Oh yes, we say. We'd love to see her dress and her hair and her jewellery.

It's out of the question, Martha keeps saying. They would never agree.

But if there is one thing we know, it is persistence.

Freckled peas

The Vestry can find no regulations that apply. In the past,
Martha might have been suspected of contracting with demons,
but the Parliament in London has repealed the law against witch-
craft. We don't know if this is because we've progressed beyond
such superstition or because all the witches have been drowned.

Martha has never been known as a fool or a liar. Once she
claimed to have seen a yellow cat the size of a two-tooth hogget
at her door, but perhaps she did, and if not, anyone could make
that mistake. Jacob complained that she sold him a calf that was
already sick and it expired within a day, but they resolved that dis-
pute between them. Mostly she has lived the way we all do, evenly,
tidily, respecting time and season. She plants oats and beans and
freckled peas on her late father's holding, keeps bees and chickens,
drives her cow to the grazings. She has no husband or children
bringing home a wage from the quarry, but then she has no one
for whom she must buy tea and sugar. She is a hard worker, if a
slow one. When she was a baby her mother, Rebecca, stumbling,
as we understand, let her fall in the hearth. In the moments it took
the parents to react, flames bit through the swaddling, gnawed the
tender infant limbs. We found Rebecca later in the church porch,
hanged dead. Martha was left with a limp and, in her breath, a
hiss as of hot ashes settling. But she is not one to make excuses.
She salts her own bacon, gathers her own turf and bark. She has
a reputation as a pickler and preserver, putting up the greater part
of her harvest and whatever she collects from woods and wastes.
She's able to sell her surplus to lazier households. She is careful

with her animals, keeping them clean and dry. In hard winters, she stints herself to feed them.

Plump and handsome

Martha is adamant that the Invisible are not the Tylwyth Teg, who are known to be short and ill-favoured.

The Ingrams are as tall as we are, she points out. Taller. They're plump and handsome.

Also the Tylwyth Teg are spiteful. They bear grudges for generations. They hide robins' eggs in shoes, crumble owl pellets into the flour.

The Invisible, Martha says, are smiling always, and if they are not smiling they are laughing. They are generous. Once I saw Miss Ingram pick up a fallen kit and place it back with its fellows.

But on further questioning, she admits such acts of charity are rare. Mostly the Invisible keep apart, chattering among themselves.

How do they dress?

It is the fashion of the city, I suppose, all bright colours and embroidery. And everything always new. Not darned or frayed or even muddy. As if every day is Easter Day.

Do any of them resemble your father? John Protheroe the smith wants to know. Or Price Price or Mother Jenkins?

But we hush him. We don't want to think that the contents of our graveyard have got themselves up in their best clothes to trot about among us, formulating opinions.

Martha shakes her head. They're not like anyone I've seen before. In looks or behaviour. I believe they're different from us altogether.

Only child

Martha's limp identifies her from some distance. It is of the lurching, stiff-legged variety, like a boat hit side-on by a swell. She uses a stick, for walking only, never hitting. When a beast jibs or straggles, she chides, like a doting granny, in a voice you could mistake for praise. She combs the burs from her cow's tail. Sometimes, milking, she seems to fall asleep with her head on Pluen's flank.

The only child of only children, since Enoch her father died, Martha has no family at all. She can breakfast at midnight if she pleases, not even trouble to prepare dinner. She has grown thinner these last years. If there were a tempest, such as our forebears talked of, strong enough to strip the thatch from our roofs and topple animals in their stalls, it might blow Martha away altogether, leaving only her shawl hooked in a blackthorn.

Enoch wanted Martha to marry Abel Pritchard. There was a conversation and a handshake and for months Pritchard would call to smoke a pipe or play chess with Enoch. On Sundays, Pritchard would walk her to church, and a comical pairing they made, Martha bobbing in the lee of his ox plod. But in the end he found a girl younger and quicker, with a dowry worth the promise. The bitterness between Enoch and Pritchard lasted until the older man's death. We do not know what Martha thought.

The Reverends

The Reverend Doctor Clough-Vaughan-Bowen comes all the way from the next county to see Martha. He lodges with the Reverend Rice-Mansel-Evans and early next morning the two men pick their way through a sparkling drizzle to the door of her cottage. Doctor Clough-Vaughan-Bowen is a learned man, of good family. He has written scholarly works, we understand, on subjects of interest to the clergy—adult baptism or the wearing of the chasuble. Rumour says he had a wife who died giving birth to their dying child. Rumour shrugs. When our neighbours and families suffer such losses we take gifts of hyssop or honey to their door, weep with them beside the new graves. But it is hard to believe that men such as Doctor Clough-Vaughan-Bowen have feelings as sharp or deep as our own. Mwynig and Brithen, we remember, bellow through the night that their calves are taken, but next day turn their inquiries instead to turnips.

The Reverend Doctor has not come to reprimand Martha, nor to interrogate her. He talks, in his educated, university English, of which she comprehends a third at most, of many invisible things. Hopes and dreams and memories. The brains of horses. The souls of the dead. The imagination. The future. The swallows sleeping snugly at the bottom of the lake.

He talks of the visible, and the traces it leaves. The fountain that sprang up where the saint pressed his thumb into the earth. The rock pierced by the giant's spear. The stony pawprint left by Arthur's hound hunting Twrch Trwyth across the mountain tops.

You see what I'm saying? he says to Martha.

Martha smiles and nods at moments where it seems appropriate.

The drizzle gives way to stumps of rainbow parting a watery sky. The reverends pick their way back and Doctor Clough-Vaughan-Bowen takes his leave, apparently satisfied.

French sauce

Martha has pressed her nose to the windows of Mr. Ingram's mansion. The Invisible dine late, she tells us, but they light neither candle nor lamp. There is no fire even, but they seem warm enough in their cambrics and silks. The ladies' throats and wrists are bare. They drink wine as red as rosehips from silver goblets. The china is blue and white, thin as a blade, and the table is laid with many dishes. They eat roast meats with French sauce, fillets and cheeks and sirloins, veal fricassey, veal ragoo, snipe, partridge, wheatears, lark livers simmered with cloves, blanched lettuce, white milk-bread, flummery and posset, clary fritters, heaped bowls of gooseberries and mulberries and quinces, sweetmeats coloured with spinach and beet and delicately fashioned into multitudinous shapes.

But who waits at table? we want to know. Who delivers the food? Who cooks it?

Martha has seen no Invisible footmen standing to attention, no butchers or vintners at the kitchen door. The Invisible, she insists, are all wealthy. There are no Invisible maids or carpenters or shopkeepers. The Invisible do no work.

But how can they live without the poor to serve them? we ask.

What about the puddings? says Eliza. Are they spiced? Do they wobble? Are they eaten hot or cold?

There are baked puddings and boiled puddings and set puddings, says Martha. Wonderful domed and turreted puddings, like palaces. Thick with candied cherries and angelica. The custard is yellow as buttercups.

They sit at table for hours, she tells us, but they talk more than they chew. They don't gobble their food or help it to their mouths with their fingers, hunting down any fragments that fall and cramming them back in.

Tell us about the meats, we say. Tell us about the cream. Tell us about the apricots and persimmons, the roast swans and haunches of venison. Tell us.

Englyn

We are enjoying a kind of fame. In other districts the gossip is of Martha. The Ingrams are mentioned in a number of sermons. The Dissenters make it yet another opportunity to talk of ale and tithes. Owen Owen composes an englyn on the subject of the Invisible that is perhaps not up to the standard of his early and most beautiful work, but we admire its wisdom, and one particularly melodious alliteration, and some of us learn it to recite to our families as we sit beside our hearths.

Markets are visibly better attended and at first we are grateful. But many of the newcomers spend only time, which they use to query and argue, cast aspersions, search behind walls and under trestles, inside calf cots and pigsties.

If anyone asks what makes us so interesting, we have no answer. We cannot explain the Invisible's curiosity. Some of us speculate it may be convenience, a matter of location. Some of us wonder if the attention is always kindly meant. Do they wrinkle their noses as they walk past us? Wave their lace handkerchiefs to clear the air? Do they avert their eyes from our misshapen bodies and pocked faces?

Mr. Ingram has a gold pocket watch. He consults it more often than is strictly necessary for someone who has no appointments to keep.

Ribbon

Some of the young people—Naomi Price and Megan Prosser and their tittering friends, plus one or two lads who are sweet on them, and Mot, the Prices' brindled cattle dog—have taken to aping the behaviour of the Invisible. They practise walking in no special direction and raising their eyebrows while others labour. They affect amazement at sickles and stooks and handlooms and potherbs and piglets. The girls have acquired a silk ribbon that they pass about between them so that one or another, usually Naomi, can wear it in her hair every day. They hold their skirts out of the mud, in the manner of Miss Ingram, and fan themselves with sprays of hawthorn.

They have developed a sudden passion for knowledge, pestering Martha with questions. She indulges them until she tires or runs out of observations, then she shoos them away like so many finches. The next day they flock back, nudging and giggling, as at their first day of dame school. Martha tuts fondly and repeats yesterday's lesson.

We think it harmless enough until they neglect their work. Three times, John Protheroe has to fetch his boy back to the forge. There is a great deal of shouting and a coulter is spoiled. Megan judges herself too good to dip rushes, while Naomi protests that stitching or churning will roughen her hands. The Prices are accustomed to their daughter's airs, but she has corrupted the once-faithful Mot, who now slinks away from his duties at every opportunity to bury his head in Naomi's knees and sigh as she folds his pretty ears into a bow.

The Ingrams should know better than to encourage such foolishness, we say to Martha. You should know better.

And when some of us point out that young folk rarely need encouragement, no one listens.

We must keep them close to home, we say.

The dog can be tied up, but our children need another solution. We give them more chores, more responsibilities, make sure they are too tired for mischief.

For a time, we think things back to normal. But the Protheroe boy wears a look of discontent as he works the bellows, and young Preece leans daydreaming on a shovel, next to the lime he should be spreading. As for Naomi, she has declared she will never marry. She would rather stay a spinster, she says, than grow red-cheeked and loose-waisted with a man whose favourite subject is the pigs he smells of. She can be seen rehearsing for her preferred future, strolling alone through marble halls or colonnades of pleached limes, her nose in the air and a frayed gold ribbon trailing behind.

Unnavigable

It is July and there has been no rain for five weeks. The summer pastures have scorched yellow, then black, as if they have combusted from within, and we bring the herds down early. The lake shrinks. Insects clump and die in its rotting margins. Springs that have never before failed run dry. When the cows complain of their multiple empty stomachs, we offer them leaves and twigs. Harvests are poor all about the district.

The Invisible are enjoying the sun, Martha tells us. They walk out at full midday to admire unclimbable heights and horrible precipices. Their hats are large. They spread cloths on the ground before they sit. They picnic on assorted meats, potted and pastried and aspicked. They do a kind of dancing, the figures intricate and indecipherable.

What is the music? we want to know. Who plays?

Martha shakes her head. There are no musicians. It is in the air perhaps. They take it with them.

Rain falls every day of September. The drops gather and hang among the grass stems until the commons are white as the floor of a shearing shed. The earth, muddled by these disorderly seasons, squanders her energies on green shoots that will not last the winter.

It turns hot again. Haf bach Mihangel. The sunsets are bronze, the dawns like unripe strawberries. The new quarry drops its prices. There is an accident in which two men die and one loses the use of his arm.

The Invisible are busy at their sports and pastimes. Not throwing or sparring or chasing a leather ball. Games with mysterious rules and objectives. Mr. Ingram covers his eyes and the others circle around him, calling and pointing. Miss Ingram gestures like a bird, or an old woman, and they all laugh. They tilt and balance and yaw and hop and fall. There is no winner. Or they are all winners. It is hard to tell.

November. The storms beat at our walls, howling accusations. When the winds drop, the bone chill starts. We count the jars, measure what's left in barrels and sacks. Every creak is a stranger creeping through the darkness with intent. December. We muffle our noses, warm our hands in our armpits. At night we hug our husbands and children close to steal their heat. The salted meat is used, the pickles and dried fruit gone. We boil hide to make broth. January. February. Those with a cow are drinking milk and praying the hay will last. Those without are living on husks and air. The Prossers have sold their bedding and only a blanket donated by the Reverend keeps their youngest from perishing.

The Ingrams must look across the lake, see our cottages dimly lit, some without smoke even. Do they imagine us huddled inside, stupid with cold, our fingers white?

In the second half of March, there is a run of dewy bright mornings. The milfyw flowers, and we put the cattle out to graze. They skip and buck like the ogre's darling children, dip their heads to the celandines to admire their bristled chins. A soft breeze strokes our hair and we hold our faces to the sun. The frogs croak all night. The sparrows get busy in our roofs and we in our beds.

But one afternoon the sky is spotted with peewits and golden plovers, fieldfares and redwings. They wheel above us, calling their alarm, then the snow they are fleeing arrives. It is the heaviest fall in ten years, heaping against walls, holding our doors closed. By morning, earth and air are so white that half a mile from us a new shore seems to have formed, before a strange, unnavigable sea. It is days before we can drive our animals to pasture, and when we do, bird corpses litter the ground, too many even for the foxes, and the grass is stewed.

When Martha limps into view we forget to ask how she is managing and instead inquire after the Invisible. How do they like the winter? Do they startle when the wind jeers from their chimneys? Do their slates seal out the thaw?

They play cards, Martha says. They enjoy jugged hare and buttered peas, sugar cakes enrobed in sugar. Miss Ingram's frock is lilac, lit from within like a spring sky.

We look at each other. We frown.

Some propose going to the Ingrams' door to beg for work or failing that last night's bones or a measure of barley. We should get up a committee, perhaps, to remind the Ingrams of their duty to their neighbours. Some even mutter of going in force. We will don dresses and bonnets for disguise, paint our faces white, light torches.

But some object. We don't need violence. Martha will help us. Let us be there when they visit, we say, as we have said before. Let us talk to them.

Tell me your demands, she says. I will represent you.

But it is not enough. We want to make our own case. We want to hear how they respond. Many of us are wiser than Martha. Many of us know more English. We will not be denied.

The Ingrams abhor questions, she says, or importuning.

We will be quiet. We will only speak when spoken to.

They cannot bear any light but that of the sun and the moon.

We are accustomed to darkness, we say.

Creaks and ventings

In the twilight borrowed from a clear night sky, we recognise our neighbours' heads and shoulders, their creaks and ventings, familiar from vigils and services. That is Widow Johns, that is Eliza, that is young Jenkin Jenkins, taking advantage of the situation to slide up close to Mary Probert. That is mice hurrying in the thatch. That is Pluen at the other end of the room, grumbling about a greasy trough or spiders in her hay. We yawn and sigh and stretch and fidget. We listen.

And finally we hear something. We think we hear something. A padding that is the approach of feet softer than a cat's, feet that make no mark on the ground. A noise as of leaves or water, gradually increasing.

Then a figure rises before us. A figure that is quite obviously, even in this dusk, Jacob, with a shawl draped over his head. He starts speaking, or piping rather, in a high-pitched voice, words that are not words in any language we know. We aren't sure what to do. Beneath his trill, an undercurrent of confusion and dismay begins.

Come along now, that's enough of that, says Old Mr. Jenkins.

Jacob keeps on babbling and chirping. He totters in a circle, flaps a lunatic hand. Almost falls over Martha stepping forward to protest, almost saves himself, staggers again, knocks her to the floor.

Then we are all up, talking at once, cheering and booing and baying, like a crowd at a hanging. Some help Martha, others pull the cover from Jacob's head. He is laughing. In a minute a rushlight is burning. Our faces glow red and orange, outraged, amused, disgusted, disappointed.

So much for your Invisible, says Jacob, cackling. And some of us cackle with him. So much for lies and nonsense. So much for anyone who thinks themselves better than us.

Martha has her face in her hands and Eliza is comforting her, turning every now and then to berate Jacob. Look what you've done, says Eliza. And some of us join in. Look what you've done. They will never come now.

Pullet

We scold Jacob until he agrees to apologise. He presents himself at Martha's cottage with a speckled pullet under his arm. She shuts the door in their faces.

Although, in the matter of Jacob's behaviour, our sympathies lie with Martha, the incident is not unwelcome to everyone. His method was crude, we admit, but he has expressed our own misgivings.

Others are confident that Jacob's stunt has only delayed our meeting with the Invisible. Next time, we say, we will be more particular with our invitations.

Martha herself seems to have aged years overnight, as elderly people sometimes do, in a sudden haste to know their end. She will not discuss the abortive visit, nor will she deliver fresh news. Tell us what the Ingrams are up to, we say. Have there been parties or excursions? A masked ball perhaps? But she will say nothing.

For a time, we make do with other topics. White peas reach double the price of wheat. Sucking pigs are 15s a head. John Johns and Ruth Prosser break their engagement and a month later mend it. Rachel Protheroe gives birth to twins. The hay is affected by mildew. In the next parish, we hear, a cow is struck by lightning and her calf bleaches white, not a shred of colour left in it. That, we think, is something Miss Ingram might wish to see. But when we say this to Martha, she turns her back.

Some point to Martha's silence as evidence of deceit. Others defend her.

It is shameful, we say, to treat an old woman with so little respect.

There must be respect on both sides, we respond.

We'd sooner listen to Martha than to mischief-makers, we say.

Fools are the best audience for foolery, we reply.

Rancour and rebuke creep among us like fleas. Friends fall out. Families almost come to blows. Some of us declare ourselves fed up with the whole business and ready to agree with anyone who will leave us in peace.

We start gathering fuel for next winter. We will stack it high this year, make a wall we cannot see over. As harvest arrives, we watch our neighbours at their crops and do not offer to help. When it is our turn, they reciprocate.

Martha has become increasingly solitary. She is gaining a reputation for rudeness. She tells the Reverend's wife to keep her baked goods to herself. She shouts at two of the smallest Prossers until they run home crying. She rarely comes to market. When we do see her, we observe that her limp is more pronounced. She stops to rest often.

Eliza brings us reports. Martha has a cough that will not mend. She is several times confined to her bed. We bring her the treats that invalids are thought to enjoy, borage tea and calves' feet. She has no appetite. We keep her fire burning, milk Pluen, feed the chickens. I'm not dying, am I? she asks, waking from troubled sleep. When she does, we will only need tell the bees.

Shadow

There is a new prime minister in London. Laws are repealed, laws are passed. Perhaps moths will benefit from the candle tax and robbers from improvements in the highways. Nobody asks our opinion. Like grass, we are meant to thrive unattended, underfoot.

We watch the road and the bridge. We look especially hard at visitors on market days. In early winter, when a light snow falls, we walk around the lake. We see prints of fox, polecat, badger. Nothing else. As we turn for home, the powder squeaks, curling our spines.

If we were rich as the Ingrams, we say, we would put up a stone drinking fountain and have our name carved on it for all to read. We would build clock towers and almshouses and schools. They would all bear our name.

Winter closes around us again. We have no heart for the seasonal festivities. We leave the wren in the hedge, the mistletoe in the trees, the mare's skull in the barn. We burn through our ramparts of fuel.

To no one's astonishment, the Prossers lose their cow. Fecklessness, we whisper. We should take them some of our own milk, a little oatmeal too. Perhaps tomorrow, we say, moving our feet closer to the fire.

When spring comes we are still alive. The day comes up a glistening mist briefly suffused with mallow. We dig and trench, plant peas and early cabbages, blister our hands and break our backs. We inspect the walls and ditches we repaired this time last year, this time the year before. Some of us patch a gap here or there, some of us shrug and stare into the distance. The sun falls through the haze like a scarlet millstone.

The Protheroe boy and Naomi Price run off in the night, gone to Liverpool, we learn, to seek their fortune in the Americas. John Preece gets an apprenticeship in Bristol. He will be his own master one day, he boasts, master of others. He will be an alderman, a mayor, with glass windows in his house and a gold chain around his neck.

We give the pigs extra barley, thinking this year we will feed them until they are too fat to walk. They will have to sit down, like little gentlemen, to take their last meal. We will kill them early, have a feast whose memory will warm us through the cold months. Chops and ribs and belly and brisket, liver and lights and blood pudding. We will eat from one breakfast to the next, saving nothing. If we need a rest, we will lay our heads right there on the table.

Sometimes, as we go about our day, a shadow falls. A blackbird clatters in unprovoked alarm. Sometimes we think we see figures on the stone bridge. They have no occupation other than leaning and an ease, leaning, that none of our visible neighbours could achieve. They are looking in our direction. We almost feel they are looking at us. We lower our eyes and walk the other way.

But at night we cannot sleep for thinking of them, across the lake, drifting on pallets of down and feather. And we wonder if they ever dream of us, or only of morning, when they will come stepping through the rushes, pocket watches in their pale hands, passing through us like a breeze through leaves, a wave through water.

Notes

Tylwyth Teg—not fair and not people
Twrch Trwyth—the cursed but well-coiffed prince boar
Englyn—a short and obedient verse
Haf bach Mihangel—the little summer that we enjoy about
    Michaelmastime, when we must pay our rents
Milfyw—the plant called by Linnaeus *Luzula campestris*; when
    it appears, we read poetry to the cows

Ade/Cindy/Kurt/Me

W HEN I was still young enough to believe that life would deliver an endless supply of people from which, if I lost some of the good ones, I could select perfectly adequate replacements, I moved, without very much forethought, to a low, flat part of the country where there was a great deal of sky to live in a poky little apartment upstairs of a poky little place called the Blue Bar (which in the interests of full disclosure should have been called the Poky Little Blue Bar), with Ade, who ran the bar, and was one of the nicest men you could hope to meet. I had been trying to make a go of it, trying to adapt myself to a subtler, more intimate geography. But after a while my old fidgetiness returned. I kept catching myself feeling nostalgic for beginnings—shivers and thrills, days when you stayed in bed for days—the very things that had often led to me behaving badly. I had to remind myself: (1) I really liked Ade (2) I wasn't paying rent (3) moving was a hassle.

I know that makes me sound shallow, but you might as well find out now that I am.

The town was very small. It had some medieval bits and pieces that it liked to boast of, a draughty supermarket with half-empty shelves, an ex-cinema that was now an ex-bingo hall, a number of overcrowded antiques shops. That was about it. The shape of the land meant there was nothing of particular interest on the horizon, nothing to aim for or be put in our places by. I liked that too.

On this particular morning, we'd been up until I don't know what small hour of the night before, but Ade woke me early, sliding over and kissing the back of my neck and saying, Hi Trish, the way he did, like he was always a little surprised to find me there under his duvet, and I said, Go away, I'm tired, and he said, in what he imagined, wrongly, was a seductive manner, You don't have to do anything, and I said, Go away, and he sighed and then he got up and brought me breakfast in bed. Because that's how nice he was.

Have you ever been with a nice man? Everyone will say how nice he is, and at first it will make you smile, Yes he is nice, aren't I lucky? But then it begins to get annoying. Yes I know he's nice, thank you. It's relentless, like there's something in their meaning that you're missing. He's so nice! And you'll think, Yes okay but he does have some faults you know. For example, he sleeps a lot. He can't stay awake through a film or a TV show or even a whole conversation. Practically every time he sits down he drops off. Plus he's rubbish at business. If he doesn't do something soon the bar's going under.

ADE

Things you need to know about Ade:

(1) He had tattoos on his arms and neck and three earrings all in the same ear and he tried to act tough and streetwise, not realising that what people liked about him was that he was harmless as a puppy.

(2) His father had been a professor of something and his mother professor of something else or maybe lecturers anyway something academic. Ade had begun a bunch of degrees but never finished any of them, dropping out of this college and that college and the other college. Long before I met him, he'd given up on the attempt altogether and decided he was a man of the soil, blue collar, dirty fingernails. He had stopped talking the way his parents did and the way he surely must have done in his private boys' school and now called everyone mate and hardly bothered to move his mouth for vowels. He'd lived on a commune keeping chickens and goats, worked as a hoddie and a brickie and a chippie (no, I don't know either), until he'd done something very bad with a router (search me) that had damaged his left eye. This meant he could not judge distance well, which is not a good thing either literally or metaphorically.

(3) He played the piano, really well. He only did it when there was no one around to listen. But I'd hear him sometimes from upstairs, in the quiet mornings, or late at night if I'd gone up before him. One of those sad old songs, 'Angel Eyes' or 'I'm a Fool to Want You', that would sound even sadder when Ade

played it, on the ancient piano in the bar with some of the keys not sounding, so every now and then the tune would halt, miss a beat, before it carried on.

(4) Number of women Ade had proposed marriage to before I knew him: three. Number of women he'd actually married before I knew him: one. Number of women he ended up marrying (to date, to my knowledge): four.

*

I did feel a bit more amiable after I'd drunk my coffee and eaten my toast with choice of jam, yes, two kinds he'd brought me, what can I say? so I went down to help him clean up the bar.

I'd done a lot of cleaning in my life and it was not my all-time favourite occupation but it was certainly easier when you were your own boss. Or Ade was your boss, which was almost better. I liked being there by myself with the light coming in sideways in that hopeful kind of way. I liked the hush that fell when I put the chairs up on the tables to do the floor, as if they were practising some secret religion.

In some ways I preferred it to what I would have said I did, if anyone asked, which was art. I was an artist, Ade liked to tell his friends, as if I was Georgia O'Keeffe, which I definitely was not. My thing right then was painting scenes on tin—landscapes or streetscapes or occasionally interiors—and then fashioning little figures and attaching them, to create these miniature worlds in which people appeared overly large and important and somewhat comic.

My friend Cindy, who had originally been Ade's friend Cindy, sold my pictures in her shop. It was supposed to be a gallery for arts and crafts and fancy design, but it had gradually expanded to include all the things shoppers had forgotten they would need as they went about their day, flip-flops and greeting cards and gloves and joss sticks and umbrellas, and now, my tinny worlds. She charged a surprising amount for them and just enough got sold to allow me to feel I was earning a living, even if Ade did give me a roof over my head and pay the electricity and the water.

After I'd done the floor I went to find Ade, but there was only a note on the kitchen table saying *Gone to Simpson's*, which meant he must have run out of something. He hadn't added a single x or o—even nice people who bring you breakfast in bed do occasionally sulk.

There was a knock at the back door and simultaneously it opened, and I knew who it would be. Cindy was always turning up at odd hours and letting herself in, like she had a right to be there. She was carrying a parcel. Wrapped in expensive handmade paper I had seen in her shop. And that was when I remembered. Fuckfuckfuck.

Where's the birthday boy? said Cindy.

He's gone out, I said.

I was flushing from the joint assault of forgetting and remembering and particularly remembering right in front of Cindy, so I turned round to hide it.

How's he taking it? Being old she meant. He was quite a few years older than me, although not, in fact, older than Cindy.

Fairly well, I said.

Did you take him breakfast in bed?

Coffee, toast, two kinds of jam, I said, turning back to face her. Do you want a cup of tea?

She looked at me sternly. Trish?

Yup.

Please tell me you didn't forget.

Of course not.

She stared me down.

We can celebrate later, I said. Come to the bar this evening. Bring your present. What is it anyway? Can we go halves?

So typical of you. (She meant forgetting.) This is why you will never hold a relationship together.

That was out of line—if people tell you their secret fears, you shouldn't slap them in the face with said fears when you have an argument.

CINDY

Cindy was tall and thin—scrawny, you might say if you were being uncharitable—with a long face and very straight blonde hair that she trimmed herself, every now and then, when she remembered. As if she rose above such things. Also, she had enormous feet. The one time we did that girly thing, trying on each other's clothes before going out—her part in which was largely to sit on the bed looking disapproving—I'd been amazed at her shoes, like dress-up shoes when you're a kid. I put them on and walked round the room laughing, saying, Just how big are your feet Cindy! Are you secretly an ogre or what!

She didn't care. Cindy never tried to be anything other than what she was. She didn't try to make people like her. She didn't smile at her customers, or anyone really, that social smile everyone does. It had unnerved me at first, but you got used to it.

As I say, Cindy had been Ade's friend before she was mine, and whenever there was any sort of tension between us—between me and her, or between me and him—she dropped me like dirt and went back to being his friend.

This was Cindy's and my relationship:

(1) She would look down her nose at the pictures I brought her, picking through them, putting aside ones she thought weren't up to scratch and telling me why, not in a tactful way at all.

(2) She would show me, by way of contrast, other things she'd got for the shop, the good stuff. She knew a lot about design, she'd gone to college as an adult, taken a degree in something visual, and she could talk your ears off about it. Look at the artless artfulness of this, she would say, picking up a bowl or a candlestick or something. Look at the texturey texture. The liney lines.

(3) She would nag me about Ade. She said I wasn't kind enough to him. If I snapped at him she'd give me a hard time for days. If I was even a bit offhand, or I teased him about his earrings, or said, Wake up Ade! she'd dig me in the ribs and hiss at me. It was hard to tell if she wanted me to leave him or marry him. She was forever going on about what a good dad he'd make, and saying he shouldn't waste his best dad years with someone who didn't want kids, and did I want kids?

(4) I would say, Why don't you fuck off and mind your own business and get yourself a boyfriend so you have something to think about other than me and Ade?

(5) We'd meet up, just her and me, once a week or so, and forget about all of the above and talk about the things that bonded us together, like how we'd left home as teenagers, and been basically responsible for ourselves ever since, and how this had made us spikey and outspoken, in a way that other people often found hard to deal with, disinclined to put up with nonsense, and unable, so far, to ever feel we quite belonged any-where. We could talk for hours, until we were either laughing or crying, and if anyone had asked us right at that moment we'd have sworn undying love for each other.

*

So that evening we were all in the bar, that is me and Ade, who was behind it, and some of his friends, Bernard and Enrique, I think, and their dog Pepper, and certainly Mohan, who was the relief barman, and maybe Vanna, it doesn't matter, they weren't my friends and they're not really part of this story, except that they were there and we were drinking shots, all of us (not Pepper), so I was already on the way to drunk when Cindy turned up and with her some foxy-faced guy who was honestly the prettiest man I'd seen in months. Maybe years.

We all looked at Foxy, a stranger, a foreigner, firstly checking to see he wasn't concealing a badge or a weapon, and secondly won-dering what Cindy was doing with him, while she was saying hello to everyone and kissing Ade and saying, Happy birthday, Nade, which is what she liked to call him, I don't know why, and not even introducing Foxy, as if she hadn't noticed he'd followed her in.

When she said hello to me, I'd have to say the look on her face was smug, although I could see she was just dying to start in on me about why I hadn't made Ade a cake or sent him up in a hot-air balloon or something.

In fact, if she'd bothered to ask she'd have learnt I was being extra nice to Ade to make up for having forgotten his birthday. I had been especially nice after he got back from the wholesalers and I was planning to be especially nice again later when everyone was gone.

So we were all there celebrating and Ade was telling stories about various awkward situations he'd got into back in his more alternative life, which everyone was laughing at although they weren't funny but it was his day and we were drinking tequila, which gets you up very quickly before it knocks you down. And this foxy guy, this pretty boy, Kurt he called himself, although I'm guessing he was born a Ron or a Jim, he had his hand up and down Cindy's leg the whole time, or if it wasn't there it was under her top, and I was thinking how can Cindy allow that? He's so blatant.

I said to Ade, See that guy feeling Cindy up? It's disgusting.

He looked at me like he wasn't as drunk as he was and said, Why do you care?

It's unseemly, I said.

But what I was thinking was, how come Cindy got the new guy? Cindy of all people? And so quickly? Like since this morning when I last saw her?

KURT

I, Cindy, am standing in my shop, my cool shop full of cool pieces that I source myself because that's the sort of cool person I am, and this guy comes in and he's like, Hey, check it out, what a cool shop. And we talk a bit, about the shop or the town, and something he says—something about where he's going or where he's coming from, something interesting anyway (not just his looks, surely, because I am above that, it would have to be some glimpse of his soul, his secret innermost self)—draws me to him, makes me look at him differently, encouragingly (although I don't smile, obviously).

He's got a thin, high-boned face, and he's faded all over, faded jeans, faded denim jacket, a T-shirt with a faded advert for coffee on it. He has those clear-water eyes that people call green, for which, perhaps, I've always had a weakness, and just looking at him, his long thighs and the coffee beans spilling over his chest, I start to think about how long it is since I've had a boyfriend or even a fuck. There was that guy up at the college, the muralist, and before that Vince from the dairy, and Winston, briefly, and Barry the Biochemist, not quite so briefly, then back in the mists of prehistory, further back than anyone remembers, there was the Fiancé, that's what we all call him, the Fiancé, as if none of us can remember his name.

And I guess Kurt was thinking some of this too, not the specific boyfriends or the Fiancé obviously, but the general gist of it, because right there, right in the shop in front of the display of cards, which I am rearranging, maybe for something to do or just because frankly I'm a bit of a neat freak, right there in front of the counter where we are having our deep or at least interesting conversation he smiles in a weird way from under his pretty lashes and he says, You have a really nice ass (ass, that's what he'd say, because he's from Texas, I think, or maybe Nevada, somewhere like that). And for a second I'm so shocked I don't even speak. And then I compliment, reciprocally, his ass, although I don't call it that.

And then, for the only time in living memory, I shut the shop, shut the shop early on the best shopping day of the week, and I take Kurt back to mine and forget all about the shop and the muralist and Vince and Winston and Barry and even the Fiancé.

And later when we're lying in bed eating tangerines, because that is all I ever seem to have in my place, a bowl of tangerines, even when you're starving hungry late at night after vodka or grass or just a hard day, and you'd really like some cheese on toast, say, or peanuts or tortilla chips, that's all there is to eat, a bowl of tangerines, artfully placed to look artless, so they must be replaced at least once a week, or more often if some fool insists on eating the bloody things. So we're lying in bed, and Kurt is smoking his Gauloises (Gauloises for fuck's sake, who does Kurt think he is?), and I say, You know what we should do, we should go down to the Blue Bar so I can show you off to my friend Trish. I call her my friend, but really she's a bit of a deadbeat and a lush and inconsiderate too, and I'm guessing a year or so from now, maybe less, we'll have entirely lost touch. Just guessing.

And Kurt turns his easy-on-the-eyes fox face towards me, and blows out some smoke and puts a hand (the one, let's say, without the cigarette in it) on my scrawny hip, like he needs to check the quality before he buys, and says, Sure babe, if that's what you want, but first . . .

*

(OK, I don't really know what happened, because I didn't ask and certainly neither Cindy nor Kurt volunteered the information. But I imagine it was something along these lines. That is, if I think about it, which actually I don't all too often.)

*

What are you doing? That was Cindy, in the bar, hissing in my ear.

Nothing, I said.

Would you stop doing it?

I'm just being friendly, I said. This was something she frequently told me I wasn't.

But here was the prettiest boy in town, who was really much more my type than Cindy's. Plus I was still annoyed with Cindy for not reminding me about Ade's birthday, which I could not believe was not deliberate on some level. That in itself justified some serious flirting. I could be charming when I wanted. I could ask leading questions, brush my fingers against someone's arm, lean in close. I could ignore glowers from whatever direction they might come, behind the bar or in front of it or even under it where the dog was sitting.

As I said already, I'm not a very admirable person. You don't have to like me. I'm not asking you to be my friend.

Some couples, even perfectly ordinary non-swinging ones, get off on watching their partners flirt. Ade and I weren't like that. It pained Ade to contemplate any suggestion that I might have or ever have had anyone other than him. Reminded him probably of wife no 1. He'd wince and look away, deny it was happening, and then he'd go all quiet because his subconscious was fully occupied with all the work of denying it and picturing it.

And Kurt, well. He'd come to the land of milk and honey, at the very least the big rock candy mountain. Two attractive women—or one attractive woman and one who could do with a trip to the hairdresser—draping themselves over him, saying, Here I am use me use me do whatever you want.

So after a certain amount of being friendly, and a certain amount of degeneration into the kind of havoc tequila wreaks, it was not difficult to cut Kurt out of the flock and shepherd him off to a quiet corner. My intention was only to enjoy a bit of appreciation and restore my self-respect, and probably to wind up Cindy a little bit. But like I say, I'd been hankering after a bit of excitement. New questions, new moves. A new person. As for Cindy, she was now behind the bar, probably telling Nade how wonderful he was, and what a loser I was.

Next thing I remember, Kurt and I are leaving the bar. I've offered to show him some of the town's landmarks. I remember reeling down the street, and I remember Kurt's arm going round me to hold me up. I don't remember any twinges of conscience.

No one likes to believe they deliberately set out to do a bad thing. There's always a way to explain it, so that it doesn't seem bad. Like, I didn't mean to do it. Or I didn't realise I was doing it. Or I had no choice but to do it. Or just, I really wanted to do it.

I want, I want. There's the sound of the icecaps melting.

In my role of tour guide, I pointed out a few of the town's not particularly interesting features. That's a bit of the old town wall. Right there behind that pub. That's the supermarket. No, honestly, it's a supermarket. That's the calvary cross. I don't know, something medieval. That's what used to be the library. Where is it you're staying again?

As we stumbled along, still holding onto each other, Kurt, who should have known that his talent was all in his looks, started talking. I didn't encourage him, I hadn't the least interest in his philosophy or his history, but he didn't seem to mind.

He was talking about growing up in Minnesota or Indiana or wherever it was. They had lived in a trailer park and his dad had worked in the Walmart and they were happy as little lambs. But when Kurt was six years old his dad had run off (although I wasn't wanting to think about Cindy right then I could see how this would appeal to her) and after that Kurt had never had enough to eat or the right shoes or sometimes shoes at all.

We'd reached the potholed car park behind the ex-cinema. Up in the sky, invisible seagulls, chased off their perches by some night monster, were flying in circles, round and round our heads, shrieking and catcalling. Kurt, oblivious, kept on talking. (Later, it occurred to me that this might have been, in fact, all he had ever intended to do with me. Talk.) After he left school, he'd worked on a farm then in the very same Walmart his dad had worked in then—I'll cut to the chase.

The best thing in his life, he said, had been his girlfriend, Annie Lou, Mary Ellen, Betty Sue, one of those folksy names. They were saving up for the wedding of her dreams when she got pregnant. First he spent weeks talking her into keeping it. And then when she'd finally agreed, or it was too late anyway, he panicked. He emptied their joint account and slunk off without so much as a note, leaving her with the unborn child and a whole bunch of lost deposits.

He said he still missed Peggy Ann and he missed the kid he'd never even seen and every day, every person he met, every place he went, he felt like he was letting them down. But what mattered, he said, was that he wasn't living a lie.

That's the most important thing, he said. You gotta be true to yourself. Without that, you don't have anything.

Then he started crying.

We sat on a wall and I let Kurt weep into my shoulder. I patted his head and felt all remaining traces of desire leave me. I was not glad he'd told me his sordid ordinary story. I was not glad that the mood was gone or that I was being saved from dancing a tango over Ade and Cindy's feelings. Mostly I was just pissed off with Kurt, not for what he'd done, but for insisting on sharing it.

But then, sitting there patting his head and feeling like slapping him, right then, for some reason, I started telling him some of my own sordid ordinary story. Perhaps the crying had unsettled me. Or the drink or the dark or the phantom bloody seagulls. Whatever the reason, I found myself telling him some things I usually skirted around or varnished over to make them prettier.

ME

For example, although it was true that I had left home as a teenager, it was not so much that I had rid myself of my parents, more they had rid themselves of me. There had been lying and stealing. Bargaining and promises and breaking of promises. There was forging of signatures and pawning of a dead grandmother's rings, a thing pronounced as particularly unforgivable. Finally there was an ultimatum. Rejection.

For example (2), when I left, I was not exactly responsible for myself, not at first anyway. I moved in with an older man, who let me spend his money without inquiring too closely on what. I was not with him for the money. But I was not with him for love either. I never liked him as much as I should have, even at the beginning, although I did enjoy the way he liked me. That did not stop me from treating him badly, cheating on him and mocking his intensity and his loyalty to me and to the ideal of love. I stayed with him far too long, turning him into someone I didn't like at all, someone watchful and brooding who devoted excessive attention to planning and executing petty revenges. Perhaps I am giving myself too much credit and I only brought out what was in him already. But it's one measure of character, what you bring out in other people. Anyway, when he finally got around to suggesting that I should leave, things had become really ugly and it would be hard for either of us to look back fondly on any of it.

For example (3): all through my twenties, while I was scraping along doing the kind of work that doesn't require any experience or qualifications, thinking of myself as an artist but hardly ever making any art (I had one job mixing paint in a factory, which seemed particularly designed to mock my floaty ambitions), I had a number of short entanglements with unsuitable people—single, attached, married, I didn't care—and left close to the same number of little messes behind me. I did not try to do this, but I didn't try to clear them up either. People seemed to me unreasonably fragile. There were worse things, I liked to tell them, than love.

For example (4): I had not talked to my parents since I left. But after a few years I started calling them, listening to the phone ring, waiting for my mother to answer, not speaking, wondering if she'd know it was me. In fact once or twice, when I heard her saying, Hello? Hello? I did speak. I hope you're happy now, is what I said. Shouted even. I hope you're happy!

For example (5): I began seeing a short, dark, rather square man who bought and sold property, something that might have given him false notions of the scope of his authority. It became obvious very quickly that what had seemed to me a beguiling confidence and decisiveness was actually a narrow and domineering nature, an intolerance for dissent. He seemed like the kind of man who might have bullied women, and if he didn't bully me it was probably only because, for the period we were together, our desires were superficially aligned. Despite all the leaving I had done, it did not occur to me to leave him, but

I did behave badly, provoking him and goading him, almost as if I wanted to see if he would actually express the violence that he always seemed on the verge of. In the end he forced the issue, late one night after a disagreement over pizza, bundling me out of his house with enough vigour to put the marks of his fingers on my arms for a week. He wouldn't wait for me even to grab my phone, which I'd been using to call the pizza. At least I had the sense to never try and go back for it.

It did not seem to me likely, at that point, that I would be able to settle down in a long and satisfying relationship, but these unhappy examples (mostly, I admit, more unhappy for others than for me) had, without my knowledge, been preparing me, priming me, for being with someone kind and loving and trying to be a little kind and loving myself. Priming me, in fact, for Ade, and when I met him, at a bus station where our tickets were configured to take us in opposite directions, it seemed he had been provided by the universe for just such a crossroads, to fulfil my specific needs and turn me into a better person.

And here I was backsliding into the same bad old stuff that I had been trying to escape.

*

Kurt didn't react a great deal to my little speech. Just, Yeah man. Wow. Sniffle.

We sat there and smoked a couple of his nasty cigarettes as the seagulls slowly settled back down.

I remembered how much Ade hated it when I smoked.

*

When I got back Cindy had gone and Mohan was behind the bar. He said Ade had crashed out in the women's toilet. I said, Isn't anyone going to get him out of there? And Ade's friends, those who were left, shrugged and looked at each other and then looked at me.

I found him laid out on the floor in front of the washbasin, drunk out of his mind. Women were stepping over him delicate as fawns.

I got down beside him and shook him a bit, not hard. Ade, I said. Are you okay?

Are you okay? he repeated. He didn't open his eyes.

You could at least have picked the men's, I said.

He seemed to have dropped off, and I shook him a little harder. Come on, I said. You can't stay here.

Stay here, he said.

*

Ade decided to pretend nothing had happened. Which of course nothing had. Exactly. It took him some effort but I was willing to help him along with it, and between us we approved a plausible version of the night in which all of us, especially Kurt, had overdone the tequila, and gone innocently wandering in the dark, bumping into one other until finally we ended up with the exact right person, like our small town performance of *A Midsummer Night's Dream*.

I'm not saying the incident hadn't put some cracks in our foundations, but I believe we could have decided they were something we could tolerate and even build our relationship on, if that was what we wanted.

Cindy was another matter.

The next day, which was a Sunday, I called her and texted her I don't know how many times and she didn't answer once. I went round to her flat and leaned on the bell for twenty minutes. I knew she was in there. She was sitting on her sofa peeling tangerines. I swear I could smell the bloody things.

The day after that I turned up at her shop and she glowered at me so hard she nearly went cross-eyed. And then began my trial and sentencing.

Audience one:

I don't want to talk to you.

I'm sorry.

Just go.

Audience two:

It's not me I'm concerned about. It's what you did to Ade. (Perhaps she believed this, but I wasn't sure that it was entirely true.)

I'm sorry I'm really sorry it was stupid. I was stupid. I'm truly sorry. (I wasn't a big apologiser so I was impressed with myself for this. I felt it was proof of my new improved character.)

Just go.

But nothing happened. Exactly.

Audience three:

It doesn't matter if anything happened or not. It's unforgivable.

Ade's forgiven me.

You think he has.

He asked me to marry him.

And you said no.

That's what you wanted me to say!

What I want is for you to consider someone other than your-self.

(Hmm.)

Are you just going to keep behaving more and more badly until you force him to reject you?

(Hmm again. I could not deny I had done that in the past. But did I want Ade to reject me? If so, what was all that effortful reconstruction about? Had I got so into the habit of endings that I could not stop myself?)

I remembered my new improved character and I took a breath and said, I want to put things right. With you and Ade.

She stared at me.

Didn't you promise we'd be friends forever no matter what? I said.

No.

It was implied, I said.

You of all people should know. Betrayal, that's the one thing I can't stand.

I'm sorry, I said again.

She kept right on staring.

I can do better, I said, although in the face of her sternest, iciest stare, I'm not absolutely sure I said it aloud.

*

When I left, we didn't lose touch immediately. I was still trying to demonstrate my personal progression and I made a point of not flouncing or sulking or slamming doors. Perhaps this made the difference with Cindy. At any rate, she softened enough to keep me, for a while, updated.

Kurt, of course, was long gone and I don't know what happened to him, but I imagine he kept on drifting east until eventually he wound up right back in Utah or Colorado, back in his trailer park and his old job at Walmart. I see him sitting beneath the vast Arizona night, on his folding chair patched up with offcuts of seat belt, weeping over Katydid and Little Kurt, and congratulating himself for not living a lie.

Ade got married only three months later, insultingly—or perhaps flatteringly—soon, to a girl called Fliss, who was, in Cindy's opinion, too uncomplicated for him. Fliss smiled continually, Cindy said, as if that was a bad thing. It didn't sound as if Fliss was hanging out trying on anybody's ogre shoes. I liked to believe Cindy might be a little sad when she thought about that.

The Blue Bar did go under and it was taken over by a big coffee chain. A lot of people thought this was the beginning of the end for the town and perhaps it was.

Ade started working at the dairy but he hated it and then he got a job at a pub probably giving free drinks to all the same old people he'd given free drinks to at the Blue Bar. He and Fliss had broken up by then.

That was the last I heard for some years, but later I met a man who had spent a summer in the town. He couldn't place Cindy but he had come across Ade, enough to know the number of his wives and that he now wore his hair in a ponytail. The man told me this as if he meant me to understand that I had had a lucky escape. That was not what I thought but it would have been too complicated to explain, would have required a long, grubby tale in which people who know nothing behave as if they have lifetimes to learn more.

We are so accustomed to stories pulled out of time and set down for us to revisit as often as we want—books, films, TV, photographs, music. It can give us a false idea about what we're doing with our lives. Sometimes I've been going about my day, dwelling on this or that, something insignificant and ephemeral, and have been jolted out of my thoughts by a bird flying by or a face in the street or the light reaching through the clouds and have found myself wanting to hit the back button. But the moment was gone, passed irretrievably into the past, and I hadn't even been paying proper attention while it was there.

Deep Shelter

F ATHER taught us to respect living things. He would not allow us to tease dogs or cats, or manhandle them, or speak, even kindly, to one that was sleeping. We knew better than to ask for rabbits or white mice, but he did let us keep the small fish we caught in the stream that ran through the woodland at the end of our road. It took twenty minutes to walk to school and two hours to meander back, across the railway and into the trees. The water was clear and cressy. It twitched with tadpoles and whirligig beetles, minnows and loach and sticklebacks. These last were my favourite. They are a fish with boldness far beyond their size. They decide on a thing then do it. The males defend their offspring fiercely, repelling even the mothers, so recently lured in with a flash of colour. Father used the proper names for their anatomies and metamorphoses. He never did have any patience with baby talk. When it became obvious that our charges were not thriving, he had us collect them up and release them back into the wild.

*

In 1951 I reached the age of eighteen, old enough for national service but not to vote. It was the year that the Festival of Britain showed us how to look forward and what we could hope to find there. The Tories loathed the whole idea. After they won the election that October, they demolished the site and threw most of it into the Thames. But that hadn't happened yet.

Mother sent me ten shillings for the festival, which she could not well afford. I was a month into my service, and while the first set of clothing was free, minor items were issued as 'slops'—that is to say, deducted from our pay. So although in theory I was paid twenty-eight shillings a week, I had yet to receive anywhere near that rate. And except for meals, the money had to cover everything, including all kit maintenance, blacking, metal polish, etc. The quality of the navy's material was excellent, I found, but the garments were not well put together. In the first week, for example, all the buttons came off my coat. Had we found ourselves at war, we'd have been running about with uniforms flapping, tripping us up and signalling our ineptitude to the enemy.

Ten shillings was a great deal for my mother at that time, because the day after I arrived at the training camp my father had set out to work and not come back. My mother had my sister, Alice, still at home, and nothing for the two of them to live on except a post office account and the chickens Mother kept in the back garden.

The only person my father had been in contact with was his brother, my uncle Walter, which we knew because Walter had written to reassure us that Father was not lying face down in a ditch, as we had feared for some days, but sleeping, peacefully or otherwise, on Walter's studio couch in Southend. So when I learned that our camp would have the chance to visit the festival, I took advantage to arrange, via my uncle, a meeting at which I hoped Father would explain his reasons and intentions. Walter wrote that I should not expect too much, which I understood to be code that my father was not yet ready to go home.

I conveyed all this to my mother, as I did not want to keep any more secrets than were necessary, and believed that in general people behaved more rationally when they had all the facts. I counselled that she should not let the news cause either fresh apprehension or renewed hope. In her previous letter she had written that the chickens were off their food and had taken to hiding themselves about the garden and panicking at imaginary sounds, and having no reason to think otherwise I assured her that they would settle down soon.

She worried repeatedly over the jobs that Father usually did, asking me which ones were urgent. The dripping tap. The rattling window frame. The loose slate that banged all night when the wind got up. Since my part in such tasks had been to do whatever Father told me to do, I found it hard to advise her. I had supposed that at some undefined date the knowledge of how a man maintained his house would be passed to me, all at once, so that I could assume the responsibilities of an adult, but he had left without warning or preparation.

Father had encouraged me to see national service as an opportunity rather than a sentence, and helped me plan the best route through it, from joining the naval cadets at school to identifying the most interesting postings for junior officers. As I mentioned, I had barely started my training when he disappeared, and potential outcomes and any part I might play in them kept running through my mind and churning it to mud. I failed inspections. I made inexplicable mistakes in radio and navigation, and even knots, which I'd been practising for years. My fellow conscripts backed away from me, as if my errors might be contagious. The officers judged me a hopeless case and saved their shouting. Everyone took it for granted that I would not pass the board and would spend the next two years scrubbing decks, without choice or variation or so much as the chance to look up and see what lay around me. I was determined to avoid this fate, but every day I felt myself a little further adrift.

I wondered what was in my father's head, whether he, too, was distracted and confused, or as calm and contained as ever. I thought particularly of when I'd seen him last, the morning I left home. He walked me to the train station, making a little speech on the way.

Seven-tenths of the earth's surface is water, he said. A man should see that for himself. A man should feel what it is to have the ocean beneath his feet and waves rolling in every direction.

I did not respond as I had no opinion, and was in any case already queasy without thinking about waves. Fortunately, he moved from watery to more general precepts.

Every experience is a chance to gain knowledge. If you cannot tell the truth, say nothing. Help others when you can, and explain your reasons when you can't.

It was mostly platitudes of this sort, although I have no doubt that he believed them, and could not conceive of a society that did not base itself on such values. When we reached the station, he shook my hand.

Good luck, John. Remember to write to your mother.

As he was departing, he turned to give me one last piece of advice.

No one respects a mumbler. Always speak up.

Then off he went, in his brown suit and brown hat, the exact colour you would choose to camouflage yourself against the dusty road.

*

With Mother's ten shillings in my pocket, I boarded the coach that had been laid on to take us to London and passed the two-hour journey practising Morse code in my head.

I had intended to stay at the armed forces club, the Union Jack, which was about half the price of anywhere else. Unfortunately, every serviceman in the country must have had the same idea, and I ended up at Clapham South Deep Shelter, a part of the Underground that had been converted into an air-raid shelter during the war and was serving as overflow accommodation during the festival. In between, it had housed those arriving from the Commonwealth with no relatives to put them up, and a very bleak first impression of Britain it must have given them.

To enter or exit, one had to queue for a narrow lift or tackle 150 feet of stairs. There was nowhere to leave luggage, and the beds, which guests had to make themselves, were narrow, short, and hard. During the hours that the Underground was running, nearby tunnels emitted a tooth-rattling roar every few minutes. In all other respects, the world above was so distant and inaudible that had it ended in a fiery Armageddon we would not have known. It was easy to believe that the victory celebrations, the demob parades and Mother packing away the blackout curtains had never happened, that instead of six years of peace we'd endured another six years of war, and that up on the surface men were running, fragments flying, homes ripping open to reveal their pathetic scraps of domesticity: a lamp, a rug, an armchair.

Within the shelter, every sound echoed and re-echoed, clanging and pealing as if the whole place were a watchtower sounding an alarm. People stomped about until two in the morning, and then again from seven on when the lights went up, leaving a scant few hours during which one could hope to rest. In addition, although many of the fittings, such as the bunks and washrooms, were primitive and rickety, the ventilation system was remarkably efficient. A cold wind blew all night, defeating the thin blanket and then the thick service coat I put over the top of it, leaving me awake to listen to a menagerie of grunts and yelps and whines, magnified and bouncing around my head.

*

The next morning, when I was making ready to leave, I discovered that during my brief moments of sleep some crook had stolen my penknife. I was sorry to lose it. While its monetary value was small, it was a decent knife and had been a present from Father.

I emerged into sunshine, feeling much as Orpheus must have when stumbling out of Hades to find that the seasons had rolled on above him. The dew was sparkling, and the trees held out their leaves like open green hands. I had some hours before meeting my father, and with no desire to return beneath ground for a train, I walked the couple of miles up to Battersea, where the festival's Pleasure Gardens were located. London was still being pieced back together, and I saw plenty of scaffolding and new construction, but also expanses of rubble and willowherb, as if the rebuilding were being approached with some caution.

On reaching the gardens, I realised that my pleasure would be rationed. Admission was two shillings, and it was another for the roundabouts or the big dipper, two for the dodgems, and so on.

I had not seen such crowds, nor such queues, since the end of the war. People of my parents' generation, the men in suits and the women in dark coats, stood stiff and upright, smiling left and right to show that they would like to join in if only they knew how, but the young had flung away their ties and jackets and cardigans and were bare-armed and bare-necked, laughing and shrieking. I myself had taken off my coat, but after shifting it from one awkward position to another, I put it back on.

Many of the rides had been brought in from the United States. Evidently, while we had been digging up roses to plant turnips and fashioning shirts out of tablecloths, the Americans had been concocting elaborate devices of fun. I was intrigued by one in particular—new to me and most others, I believe—a vertical cylinder revolving at speed, whose floor dropped away to leave its riders pinned to the walls, looking like trickery to those who failed to understand the principles of centripetal force. All the girls screamed like souls in torment, and one fainted and had to be carried out afterwards. When I rode in it, I found that it was not very comfortable, and at the conclusion I had to sit by the fountains for some minutes.

One curious effect of my father's disappearance was that I saw him everywhere, in a familiar stride or gesture, a certain tilt of the head. On this occasion, it was the way a man clasped his hands behind his back. I approached him but knew, even as he turned, that he was a stranger. He seemed affronted, as if I were accusing him of something shameful, and I hurried away, feeling foolish. I had recently written to Mother about this very tendency, warning her that the heart, or rather the mind, will deceive our eyes if we let it.

I took the bus to the main exhibition site, where another admission claimed five of my remaining shillings. The Telecinema would have cost a further shilling, so with regret I crossed it off my list. In any case, I was preoccupied with the rendezvous to come. I practised what I imagined were manly phrases. Now look here, old chap, we really must put an end to this nonsense. I say, my good fellow, we simply cannot allow this shabby state of affairs to continue. That sort of thing.

We had arranged to meet at the Skylon, chiefly because it was easy to find. It was supposed to symbolise our sparkling aluminium future, but to me it looked like a remnant of the war, a slim barrage balloon standing on its tail. Whenever my gaze hit on it, I thought first of my father and then of the sound of planes in the night.

I spotted Uncle Walter immediately, and as I neared I could not avoid acknowledging that he was alone.

He's not coming, he said. I'm sorry, John.

It was the first time anyone involved in the dismal situation had apologised.

Perhaps Father had made the appointment in good faith, but on further reflection he had decided not to keep it. Did not wish, probably, to be questioned or held to account. I recalled the expression of the man I had accosted earlier.

I must see him, I said. We simply cannot allow this shabby state of affairs to continue.

Walter raised his eyebrows, and I reminded myself that I was eighteen years old and almost qualified to defend my country.

We really must put an end to this nonsense, I said. Let's go back to Southend right now.

He's not staying with me any more, Walter said in his even voice, so like my father's. He's decided to move on. He's leaving London today.

Where is he going?

He asked me not to tell you. If you want to contact him, you may send a letter to me, and I will forward it.

My practised phrases fell away.

I don't agree with his decision, Walter said, but I feel I must respect his wishes.

I asked if Father had given any reason for his actions, and Walter said no. I asked if a woman was involved, and he said he thought not. I asked if Father's leaving was temporary, and again he said he thought not. I asked if he knew Father's plans, and he said he did not. I asked if, indeed, Father had any plans, and my uncle paused for a long moment, then said he didn't know.

Father used to say that human beings are a mystery and you never truly know even those closest to you. It has since occurred to me that perhaps he meant this not as observation but as warning.

Walter stood frowning at his shoes. He was not only my uncle but also my godfather. He had taken an interest in my schooling and had always remembered my birthday, even during the war, when he was having his own difficulties. He looked up at me.

I imagine he will visit some of the exhibits before he goes.

*

The Land of Britain was mud and swamp, life compressed into fuel. I passed by, knowing my father would not linger there, and pushed on through the arrival of farming, the growth of towns, steam, industry, production, until I reached transport. Gleaming motorcycles and cars primed to spring from their plinths and out onto roads not yet imagined. Crowds of men stood reverent, but he was not among them.

I moved on to the Dome of Discovery. It was like stepping into a giant spacecraft that interplanetary visitors or our future time-travelling selves had docked beside the Thames. The exhibits celebrated Britain's mastery over mountain, sea, desert, ice, sky, outer space. In the polar section, a team of bored huskies turned cold eyes on the throng. And there, gazing right back at them, was Father.

He was hatless, his hair noticeably longer, curling about his head in an eccentric fashion, and he wore not his brown suit but a darker one, without a tie. It struck me as odd that he would have left his family to go out shopping for clothes, but then I thought perhaps the suit was Uncle Walter's—it did have the look of something made for a taller man.

He did not seem surprised to see me, nor sorry, nor pleased. We shook hands like old acquaintances and went to the nearest of the cafés for a cup of tea.

It's most impressive, all this, he said, once we were seated. Quite a show. He sounded like his usual self.

For several minutes, we talked of trivia—the festival, the weather, my officers and fellow recruits, the shocking price of everything in London—until I interrupted an anecdote about mint sauce to ask him to explain himself. He was my father and it was not my habit to confront him, so I was nervous, and perhaps I fluffed my line. At any rate, he looked at me, then laughed, not unkindly, but with a fleeting puzzlement, as if he did not understand my question but did not mind too much.

How is your mother? he asked. It was his first mention of her.

She is well, I replied, but very anxious. And emotional.

Is she? This was news to him, it seemed.

She baked three candles in the oven last week, I said. She had to scrape the wax out with a knife.

It's a difficult time for her, he said, both of us leaving at once.

I stared for a moment or two, but he showed no trace of discomfort.

I was called up, I reminded him. I had no choice.

And how is your sister?

Alice is anxious too.

I hope she is doing well at school?

Yes. Top of her class.

He nodded. I believe that the neglect of women's education is among the most significant challenges facing our country.

He offered this as revelation, but I had heard him on the theme many times before. I tried to reel the conversation back towards more immediate problems.

In situations like these, I said, girls are often forced to leave school.

He switched abruptly to another of his pet subjects, the theory that humans should eat only fruit and honey and nuts and such limited portions of animal protein as wandering nomads might happen upon, avoiding cereal and milk especially. At Walter's, he said, he had adopted a strict new regime, and to this he attributed the fact that his knees no longer bothered him.

I thought his evidence insufficient but did not say so. You could follow such a diet anywhere, I said.

He looked at me, and changed topic again. You still take an interest in science, I'm sure, he said, as if we had not seen each other for years.

Of course.

Do you know that they have equipment here that allows

you to observe a radio signal transmitted to the moon? That's something worth seeing.

I had to agree with him.

We are on the brink of marvellous achievements, he said. Electronic brains and mechanical men. The end of disease and starvation. This will be a golden age of discovery.

I have heard that.

I do wish I'd been born forty years later. He appeared to think this a perfectly reasonable desire, forgetting, perhaps, that it would erase the births of his children. I should like to experience it all. This century and the next.

My concern is this month and the next, I said. What should I tell Mother?

How many of us decide our own future?

I wasn't sure whether he expected me to answer this.

He put his hand to his heart, in the manner of one about to make a declaration of deep importance. But instead he said, You know, John, I'm not feeling quite myself.

He did look pale.

Are you ill? I asked, thinking this would explain a great deal.

Perhaps a glass of water would help, he said.

I'll fetch one for you.

No, no, he said. I'll go. You wait here.

I protested, but he was already up. As I said, he was my father, and it was my habit to obey him.

I watched him walk away. Among the crowds and the shadows between them, the dark suit blended in better than his old brown one would have.

I waited fifteen minutes, ample for him to make his escape. Then I went back to the exhibition.

That afternoon, I resolved to stop trying to be manly and to start taking some responsibility. When evening arrived, instead of boarding the coach and returning to camp, as I was required by law to do, I hitched to my mother's. It took nearly four hours, so I had plenty of time to ponder the consequences and how I would face them.

*

For years, Alice and I sent Father, via Uncle Walter, news of significant events—graduations, marriages, births. Walter assured us that the letters were received, but not once did we hear back, and gradually we stopped.

When Mother died, in 1987, I wrote to Father again, as I supposed he should be told and did not know how else he would find out. And again I had to ask my uncle to forward the letter. In a matter of days, Father replied—our first contact in nearly four decades. He said he was sorry to learn of her death, though it must have been a happy release from suffering. (It did not seem to occur to him that he might have been a cause of that suffering.) He also said he believed that death is not a reason for alarm or grief, that life is like electricity, passing on to light up another bulb when the old one is worn out or broken.

He revealed that since leaving London he had been living in Spain. He said that the climate and character suited him well and he had never regretted going south, although his roots and sympathies remained in Britain. He did not explain what he meant by that. Then he wrote for three pages of the minutiae of his daily activities—his garden, his bees, the weather, the melting snow in the mountains, local wildlife, his favourite radio programmes—with not a single question about me or Alice or any of his grandchildren. He did say that when he listened to the BBC it awakened nostalgia and memories, as of another existence. And I think this is how he viewed the period of his life that we had shared: like the experience of another person, not intimately connected to him.

He signed the letter 'sincerely', as if unwilling to offer even the most formulaic expression of love. Just 'My best to your family. Sincerely, Dad' (not a name I had ever used for him). In the margin he added, 'Will you pass on my best to your sister?'

In the course of the letter, he told me, too, that he would send his address when he was settled. When he was settled! He'd lived in that village for more than thirty years, most of it in the same house. He'd planted peach and apricot trees in the garden, some of which were two feet round the trunk when he died. I know this because Alice and I visited afterwards, to see to his few affairs.

From Mother we had inherited, in addition to some savings bonds and a surly cat, a vast quantity of ephemera: snapshots and postcards, pictures that Alice and I had drawn, school reports, examination certificates, invitations to weddings and christenings, photos of the grandchildren, Christmas and birthday cards. But Father left nothing. He had no relations in Spain

that we could trace—all our speculation about a second family
had been false—no money, scarcely any possessions, no photographs or letters or other evidence of human relationships. His
neighbours told us he'd mostly kept to himself.

*

I never did replace the stolen knife. Father had given it to me on
a family camping trip, showing me how to whittle with it, how
to splice a rope and pick a horse's hooves. He gave Alice a book
about the seashore, and helped her identify cockles and whelks
and edible crabs. With these gifts, we could have survived a day
or two, perhaps, if he'd left us there alone.

The campsite was behind a beach in Cornwall, with pines so
thick around and above that even by day it was dim and shad-
owy. The scent of conifers always reminds me of that holiday.
Mother, as usual, kept snapping away with her camera. I often
look at those photos now. Several show the site. 'Our camp',
she wrote on the back of one, and 'Another view of our camp'
on another. There is just one of her. She is twirling on the sand,
like a girl, arms outstretched and head high, a wide smile on
her face. 'Don't I look a duck?' she wrote. Most are of Alice and
me, playing or swimming or eating or squabbling. In the back-
ground, my father stares out at the waves or walks away from
us along the beach or leans on the trunk of a tree, his back to
the camera, gazing at a horizon only he can see.

In fact, aside from their wedding album, I don't think I've
seen a single picture of my father's face.

*

I am an old man now. I have outlived my wife and my sister and one of my sister's children. I have done no great harm, I believe, but certain small and repeated unkindnesses lie so heavy that on wakeful nights they can stop my breath. When I think about what is to come for me, I do not look far ahead. When I think about what is to come for those I will leave behind, I am afraid.

That day in 1951, before I set off to hitch home, I returned to the Dome of Discovery. I studied displays on nebulae and red giants, feeling a calming of my emotions in the contemplation of unimaginable remoteness. Finally, I found the demonstration Father had mentioned. A cathode-ray tube showed how a radio signal, transmitted from the site, reflected off the moon and returned to us two and a half seconds later. It was simple and effective, an almost tangible representation of the powers we could harness, the distance we could travel.

That was the future, we thought then: the stars, the galaxies, outer space. The things we feared were not quite the same as those we fear now. We believed that we had managed to hold civilisation together, against the odds and at huge cost, and that it was still under imminent threat from any number of destructive forces. We worried about war and plague and revolution; the next ice age; the end of Empire and empires; and most of all, a single, impetuous moment that would trigger catastrophe: radiation, mutation, our species surviving, if at all, as a deformed, damaged version of what we had been.

Only the advancement of knowledge could save us. Science would build the machines that would allow humanity to step out into the solar system and beyond. The petty grievances of the earth would be dwarfed by the new adventure. Our world would finally come to seem—perhaps during my life, perhaps even by the end of the century—a noisy, crowded place where we had passed a little time before moving out into the grand, airy habitations of the universe.

Work

A WHILE back, when things were not going smoothly for me, this guy I knew, Paul, bought himself a restaurant, and when it was still pretty new and he'd spent all his money on forks and skewers and real people who knew how to run a restaurant, he asked if I would help out, and I said yes because I didn't have a job and I didn't seem capable of getting a job and I didn't have a clue how to turn my life round and point it more in the direction I had expected it to take.

I'll pay you, of course, he said. But I'm afraid it won't be very much.

And it was in fact a pittance that it was probably illegal to hire someone for, which was why it made sense to hire me. Later when I thought about it, and about how amazingly well the restaurant did, I thought he could probably have paid me more but I suppose that's how he got to be rich and I didn't.

I don't know what I had imagined I would be doing, perching on tables with a little notepad or making frilly garnishes out of lemons. But what I actually did was the things everyone else was too qualified to do, like mopping the floor and cleaning and then mopping the floor again and fetching and carrying and most of all washing up. And if you don't know I can tell you, washing up in a restaurant is hard. It's like going under with the Titanic, only hot. The dishes come crashing in around you and steam billows up in great clouds and sweat drips down you like rain on a window. I swear there must be a big room in hell which is just washing up and nothing else where they put all the people who didn't like to get their hands dirty.

I realised right on the first evening that this wasn't going to be any fun, but once or twice while I was still in the middle of realising it Paul smiled at me in a harassed sort of way and said Good girl, as if I was a dog or ten years old. I'd thought that the part of me that was meant to look into the future and want things was dead and gone, but there was obviously some little scrap of it still alive and nursing a teeny crush on Paul. So I wiped the sweat off my eyebrows with the back of my sweaty hand and tried to look sophisticated and sexy and indispensable all at the same time.

Actually, I didn't get to see much of Paul, who spent most of his time Front of House, as he liked to say, selling expensive bottles of wine, which, as I found out when I was working there, is how restaurants make their money. Mostly I saw Gareth, who was the under chef, or Sous Chef as they would say, which is just under chef in French, which meant he spent all his time skinning things and gutting things and chopping things.

Gareth didn't complain. Gareth was a dopehead. He was lucky to have a job at all.

In fact, when you think about it, everyone there was lucky to have a job, and maybe Paul was actually some kind of a secret good Samaritan and the restaurant was a place he made so that people like me and Gareth could be safe for a while.

Whenever we got the chance Gareth and I used to sit out by the dustbins smoking, and we got to be friends, as much as two people like us could be at any rate. And what happened was we somehow formed ourselves into a kind of alliance against Paul, who was The Boss and therefore different from us. And Gareth said that this was a deep biological instinct, like monkeys or wolves or communists. I did feel a little guilty, but after all Paul was still paying me the pittance and he wasn't even noticing me except sometimes to stick his head out the back and say, Leave Gareth alone will you? He's got work to do. Which was insulting in at least two ways that I can count.

We were working what was called Split Shifts, which meant you did one shift in the day and one shift in the evening and in between was about two hours of free time to do absolutely anything in the whole world you wanted to do.

The early shift was usually quiet. Not that there wasn't loads to do, getting everything Prepped, as they liked to call it, for Service, but in the day you could take a lot of breaks and Paul wasn't always there and the chef, Marcus, who was the boss of all of us except Paul, and even a little bit of him too, was often busy planning menus or chatting up suppliers or whatever, which meant you got more of a chance to sit out back in the cool.

Gareth was older than me. He had that shrunk-in-the-wash look of people who've been too busy taking illegal substances to eat. He always spoke very quietly and he used to do this funny little giggle, usually when there was nothing funny that anyone else could see. But it was good that he could find something to laugh about. Also, he talked, in that quiet voice, more than almost anyone I've ever met, including twelve-year-old girls. On day one, when I barely knew him at all, he told me practically his whole life story, which is a thing that I have noticed with people who take a lot of drugs, they have no discrimination, they don't distinguish between their intimate friends who'd hold their head and their hands and their hair for them and someone who just happens to be sitting next to them scrounging their rollups.

One part of his life history that Gareth told me that day was about his childhood. His mother died when he was very young and he went all over the world with his father, who was something to do with the war against TB, which sounded pretty important to me. But Gareth said it was actually a little spat that distracted people from the True Struggle. And it meant Gareth got moved about from place to place like luggage and never had a home. And I thought all that moving might have added to his ordinary dopehead lack of discrimination, because another kind of people who can't make friends properly, I have noticed, is people who've travelled a lot.

Another part of his life history that he told me that day was about a girl he'd been in love with. She was his soulmate, he said. When he knew her she was very sad, for reasons I couldn't quite grasp, but fuck knows there's enough bad things out there happening to someone, try making a list, it's a wonder there's anyone left who isn't sad.

He used to send her poems and put flowers through her door and she treated him very kindly, like a little brother. She had all these suitors and ex-suitors that she was too sad to go out with, but she liked to have them around her. That sounded weird to me but he saw nothing wrong with it, except that it made him unhappy. And he got more and more unhappy and eventually he took an overdose. He woke up in hospital and this girl would come and sit with him and they wouldn't speak at all but she understood him, so he thought, anyway, I have my doubts. But you can form an idea like that, that there is only one person and one time and one place where you could live, and then for the whole of the rest of your life you'll feel homeless.

He told me about all the jobs he'd done too. He'd worked as a postman for a while, but it involved a lot of rules, and he'd got sacked for emptying the postboxes in a different order, which it turns out is about the worst thing you can do if you're a postman. Then he'd been a delivery driver, until one day he was on the motorway, and a lorry pulled out, and a car cut in, and it was okay, nobody crashed or anything, but he realised he was basically spending his days in a race to the death. So he came off at the next exit and turned the van round and took it to the beach. Then he'd got a job in an electronics factory. Most of the other people were women because the job involved putting together fiddly little things, which they do better with their small hands. And that suited him very well because there was music playing and you could talk. But then the company found a way to do it cheaper using machines or desperate small-handed children in another country. They asked for voluntary redundancies, so suddenly everyone thought someone else should go, the older ones or the younger ones or the single ones or the married ones, depending who was thinking it. They turned against each other, which Gareth said was how Capital kept people in a state of semi-consciousness. After that he'd got his first job in a kitchen, and he liked that well enough, there was no driving and he thought it would be difficult to come up with a machine to replace him.

As it turned to winter it got chilly but we still sat outside when we could. On the whole, it was going okay for me. Another thing I didn't know before and only found out while I was there, is that when you're doing that kind of work and you're so tired at the end of it that you haven't got the strength to keep up your usual barriers, you get close to everyone pretty quick and you get a warm glowing feeling towards them, as if they were your actual friends. So there was that, and then I was sort of getting used to the split shifts, more or less, and by now I'd given up on Paul being anything other than The Boss, and the tiny pittance was making a tiny nibble into the big pile of debt I'd accumulated. Plus, most of all, I was starting to feel like maybe I could be a person who could hold down a job. And that was quite a leap forward for me.

When I say about this warm feeling, it wasn't like that with everyone of course. There were some people you just couldn't stand, and for Gareth and me it was the chef, Marcus. People come and go in kitchens, but Marcus had been there from day one and didn't look like leaving any time soon. Of course, as I said before, he got to boss everyone around, so it was a good job if you're the sort of person who likes that. And he was.

Marcus was older than all of us, with grey hair, and he had that look some men have of seeming to have a moustache without actually having one, which I have always thought makes a person seem sly and untrustworthy. He was an alcoholic or maybe an ex-alcoholic. And he was very tall and what you might call gaunt. It's funny that we were dishing out all this cream and butter and treacle pudding but everyone who ever worked in that kitchen was skinny as a dog in a war zone and looked like they were starving right there in the middle of all that food, like there was some enzyme required for normal living that their body couldn't process.

Marcus was a bit of a tyrant, but it turns out it's practically obligatory that the chef should act like a sergeant major or the teacher that everyone hates. And of course I was so lowly he didn't speak to me that much.

But Gareth was Marcus's second in command, his Sous Chef, and Marcus ordered him about like his very own personal Sous Dog. And Gareth said Yes Chef, no Chef, three bags full Chef just as promptly as anyone, but when he was out back he would sometimes be simmering, you could see it, all worked up so he had to sit with his eyes closed, humming.

Gareth never argued or complained or sulked or even twitched an eyebrow, but there was this one thing he would do that you could see really got to Marcus. It was pretty much a rule there that everyone got in early. It was part of the whole thing where we were all supposed to be sucking up to Marcus like all we'd ever wanted was to wear his fancy hat. But what Gareth would do was turn up early and then sit down on the wall opposite the restaurant and just wait. All of us, including Marcus, would have to walk right past him. Then right on the dot, Gareth would come in, not even half a second late, so Marcus couldn't say anything at all. And you could see it ate him up. And then he'd shout at Gareth a bit louder during the next service, and then Gareth would have to keep his eyes closed and hum a bit longer, and on it went.

So it got to be December, and some people had left and some new ones had come, and one of the new ones was Nish. She worked there part-time, when her ex could have the kids, and she was one of the sweetest people I've ever known. She was a recovering anorexic—she said she was recovering, although I never saw her eat—and she looked as if she'd snap in two if you touched her and also she had scars on her arms from where she used to cut herself with knives and scissors and probably the whole Batterie de Cuisine. She said she didn't do that any more, so there you are, people do get better sometimes.

Gareth liked Nish. Which meant, it turned out, that when she was around he hardly spoke, so you started to see where he'd gone wrong in his former relationships. He did, however, at some point pluck up the courage to say something to her and she said, No way no, you're kidding aren't you? only more kindly than that I'm sure. She told me afterwards that what with the kids and the job and the ex and some guy who came over sometimes, she had quite enough to take care of already.

Gareth didn't say anything about it, but you saw him sometimes looking at her quite mournfully.

So Gareth and Nish and I were out back one day. It was getting towards Christmas, lots of office parties wearing paper hats and tinsel like they were taking part in some kind of ceremony. They laughed a lot but they looked scared out of their minds, of what I don't know, of what they were laughing at, or the people they were laughing with, or how another year had gone by and here they were celebrating it. Anyway, they made a lot of extra work for us, throwing silly string and ordering everything in sight because they weren't paying for it, and we were all even more tired than usual and most of us weren't exactly looking forward to Christmas.

So when Marcus came out telling us to quick march into the kitchen no one felt much like moving and he had to come out again. And probably because she was the most timid of us, he started on Nish. Do you want this job or not? he said. And you could see she was going to jump up and go in, and normally that's what we'd all have done. But maybe because it was Nish, or maybe because it was Christmas, or maybe because of the True Struggle, Gareth put his hand out to stop her and said, We're taking a break. We'll be in in a minute. He didn't even say Chef.

Marcus looked taken aback for a second because no one ever ever ever answered him back and then he said, You'll be in when I say.

We'll just be a minute, said Gareth.

You've had warnings, said Marcus. Which was news to me.

Gareth didn't say anything and Nish and I didn't know what to say.

Maybe none of you want this fucking job—that can be arranged, said Marcus, and he turned round and walked back in and after half a second Gareth got up and said, This isn't on, and followed him in. And Nish and I looked at each other and she said, Oh shit. And then we went in too.

We could hear Marcus shouting in the cold room, with silences that must have been Gareth answering very quietly. I thought it might be a good idea to give the floor another mop and Nish started on the veg. Then Paul came in and wanted to know what was going on and everyone just looked at each other and said nothing and Paul went into the cold room and very soon after that all three of them came out of the cold room and went into the dining room in single file, Paul first and Marcus last with Gareth in the middle and no one saying anything any more.

I never found out if Gareth was sacked or if he resigned. I asked Paul and he refused to discuss it. He's not coming back, he said, and that was all he would say. I asked for Gareth's phone number but he wouldn't give it to me, so I had to go into the office when he wasn't there and look for it. There wasn't a phone number, only an address, so I wrote it down on a page I tore out of Paul's desk diary, which was blank and just for show or because someone imagined it was the kind of thing you would need to run a business, which wasn't true, it seemed to me, obviously what you needed was a cold hard heart.

A couple of days later, between shifts, I went to the address I had copied down. I had to take two buses to a bit of town that was probably nice when Queen Victoria was on the throne and which hadn't been repaired or even cleaned since. Everything was slumped, and some of the windows were boarded over and most of the rest were covered with that thick grey dirt that takes years to build up.

Gareth lived on the top floor of a place that had about ten doorbells although it didn't look big enough for that number of fully grown people. I rang the bell with his name under it and when nothing happened I rang the rest of them but no one answered, so either they were all out at work which didn't seem likely or they thought I was the bailiffs or the social or someone else who might want to prise them out of the hole they'd managed to wedge themselves into hoping to wait it out until the tide came in.

But then this woman opened the door, not to let me in, but to come out herself. She had shopping bags full of stuff that was not shopping, and no teeth, real or false. She looked at me suspiciously, but probably she looked at everyone that way, it wasn't that she recognised me as one of her own.

I went past her through the open door and up the stairs to the top, where you had to stand one step down and reach up to knock on the door. I hammered away for a while and I shouted that it was me. And that was the end of my ideas. But then I heard a shuffling inside, and Gareth opened the door. And he looked so pleased to see me, I felt bad for not being more pleased to see him.

He looked like he'd aged ten years. He hadn't shaved, and his eyes were red, and he was wearing pyjamas with an old, worn coat over the top, like one of those shell-shocked convalescing soldiers out for a walk in the grounds.

We went into the kitchen, which was also I suppose the sitting room, it had a couch in it, which we didn't sit on, but no table. Do you want a drink? Gareth said, but he looked anxious when he said it which made me think he might not have anything to drink, or not enough to give away at least. I was standing next to the cooker and there was a pan there with some soup in it, a bit of thin soup which didn't look like it would nourish a dormouse.

I asked if he was alright. He looked at me like he was still listening to bombs exploding somewhere off in the distance. I told him what had been going on at work, how upset Nish had been, what Marcus and Paul and everyone had been doing. He said some things which seemed unconnected. I talked about the bus journey. And the weather. Asked what he was going to do.

It seemed that everything we had talked about together, that had been like a cosy blanket we were knitting between us, each of us with a pair of needles, clickety click, all of it had been left behind the bins, and we had to start all over again.

Then Gareth said, You're a kind person. Which I knew I wasn't. And he came over to me and leaned, keeping his feet in place, just leaned, until he was resting his head on my shoulder. And I didn't know what to do but I felt panic coming up in my throat like moths so that I couldn't speak. Him leaning on me in this way, as if I could possibly bear his weight, as if I could stay upright under it, as if I wouldn't fall over into the dormouse soup at any minute, was intolerable. I had to stop it.

You'll be fine, I said, which was patently not true. He kept leaning and I said I have to go now, I have to get to work. And the word landed at the end of the sentence with a thud, as if I was rubbing it in that I had somewhere to go and he didn't.

He did a kind of reverse lean then, lifting his head off my shoulder and returning to perpendicular, and he stood in front of me, in his pyjamas and his coat, swaying a little.

You'll come again, yeah? he said.

Of course, I said. I mean, if I can. Of course.

And of course, I didn't. And in fact I never saw or heard of him after that. And even now it makes my stomach hurt to think about what might have happened to him and to know I didn't help or even try to help but just went back to Paul and Marcus and mopping the floor, as if there were sides and I'd picked one.

I kept working in the kitchen for quite a long while after that, until hardly anyone remembered I hadn't always been there, and half the time I hardly remembered myself. Nish left, and other people left, and even Marcus left in the end. But whoever was there, however things changed, somehow it very quickly felt to me like it had always been that way, and always would be.

Gareth wouldn't have been surprised by that. He used to say that work is like dope. The Dope of the Masses he used to call it. Sometimes it makes you high, and sometimes it makes you sick. But mostly it just softens the edges, so you won't wonder how to use your days, or notice that they're passing.

Butterflies of the Balkans

Vienna

T HEY had planned to pass swiftly through the imperial
city, which held nothing of interest for them, but they
were delayed by Prue's friend, Mr. Jolley, who neither arrived
nor answered Prue's cables. At night, uniformed maids rustled
forth to polish gilt petals and plaster leaves and Dottie dreamt
of insects emerging from the empty air to cluster at sculpted
flowers. She wondered what weary Methuselah had put it about
that patience would expand with age.

On the third day, over a dowager's breakfast of soft rolls and
tart jam, Mr. Jolley's response came, stripped of those parts of
speech that might mellow it.

Regret stop. Important matters stop. Something something.

I'm sorry dear, said Dottie, I didn't catch that last part.

UNABLE TRAVEL STOP! boomed Prue.

There's no need to shout, dear. Increasingly Dottie found loud
voices more trying even than quiet ones, consonants buzzing at
her one good ear.

As Prue began to dissect Mr. Jolley's explanations, Dottie took another spoonful of cherry preserve. In truth, other than the wasted days, she was not sorry. She did not like to think ill of anyone, but Mr. Jolley had kept a wife and at least one child propped by the fire in Cirencester as he went trotting about the world with The Honourable Prudence Hawtrey.

Then, too, Dottie had found that she met with a more courteous reception when travelling without a gentleman companion, a happy consequence, perhaps, of Queen Victoria's long and lonely reign. Past a certain age, all British ladies were so indistinguishable from the late empress that, to avoid any potential faux pas, officials of remote places would offer a grey-haired butterfly collector in long skirts the very same welcome that had been set aside in case the monarch herself should happen to drop by.

Mr. Jolley's news had undone some stiffening layer in Prue's construction. She drooped as they made their way to the station and settled into their compartment. Even as the train started to move, on that cloud of shouts and whistles and steam so intoxicating to any traveller, she only sank deeper into her corner. Dottie hoped this did not bode ill for the expedition, their first together in a long acquaintance conducted, until five days earlier, largely through correspondence.

Edwin's wife has never liked me, said Prue, as they passed through Vienna's grubby fringes. But she'd do well to remember I knew him first. I have some title. After which she fell asleep almost instantly and remained so for most of the twenty-six-hour journey, her mouth open and her snores rattling even above the grind and clatter.

Dottie did not sleep herself, not because of the noise, not because of the discomfort, not because of having to change trains at Brod in darkness so complete they had to light matches to find their seats, and not because of people popping in to inspect their papers or offer them coffee and boiled eggs or just to gawp and snigger and pass an unsolicited opinion. Dottie had slept the sleep of the innocent through thirty years of marriage and motherhood and, other than some wandering bleak months after her husband died, all the years since. In her widowhood, Dottie had slept on trains in France and Italy and Spain and Austria. She had slept in shepherds' huts in the Pyrenees and refuges in the Alps and tents in the mountains of Lebanon. She had slept in the open, rolled in a horse blanket, next to a fire, a small woman surrounded by large men, each with his weapon of choice at his right hand. But she did not sleep on the journey from Vienna. Instead she counted the hours, and went over her plans, and thought about the fly in King Herod's ear. Many people, she had observed, not only accepted but welcomed the handicaps of age, as if they were just deserts for all the small or large faults committed in their lives. Those people, she thought, had too little to do.

Sarajevo

Sarajevo was a gracious prospect of low walls and enclosed courtyards, studded with cypresses and slender minarets that seemed on the verge of unfurling sails and lifting the whole city into the air to float free of its earthly troubles.

They put their luggage down, splashed cold water on their faces, and took themselves directly to the museum to seek out Dr. Lakić. A slight man in European dress, he spoke excellent German, good English, and passable Italian, but Dottie struggled with his soft voice and his accent.

He led them through the building, dismissing rocks and pots and bones with a wave to left or right. When they reached a room lined with glass cases, he turned and opened his arms, smiling.

Clouded yellows. Purple-shot coppers. Sooty satyrs. Scarlet underwings. Apollos and swallowtails. Queens of Spain and Dukes of Burgundy. Tiger blues and marbled skippers. Silverwashed fritillaries and pearly heaths.

Dottie adored her children, all grown into fine men and women, excepting perhaps Ralph, the eldest, who seemed to have forgotten all the thrift and charity he had been taught. She missed her husband every day. Still, what it would be to have back twelve months, twelve weeks, even twelve days of that time to devote to the study of butterflies. The field was so various and vast, and her forays into it had been so limited. It would be unjust if she were to be halted by her treacherous, ageing body.

She had learnt to negotiate deafness and cajole her rusting joints into motion. But now some mischievous artist was taking an eraser to her vision, removing a spot here, a patch there, whole strips around the edges. In poor light, particularly, or when she was tired, objects could arrive unannounced, beside her or even right under her feet. She had not told anyone, most especially not her children or her physician. Nature, she had observed, had a capacity for self-healing. She was not a tractor. But examining the museum's collection, she could not deny there was some deterioration. She reminded herself that she had barely slept in two days.

Their plan had been to travel east the next day, to the mountains of the border region, where they might hope for some of the most interesting species and perhaps some rarities. But the news Dr. Lakić imparted was not good. Incidents at a frontier post, a man shot, two men, no one was sure, so many rumours. An Austrian, or a Turk, or a Bosnian. A smuggler, a shepherd, a soldier, something something. His voice sank to a murmur.

I beg your pardon?

INSURGENT, Prue trumpeted in Dottie's ear.

And besides, Lakić went on, the season is late, perhaps as much as . . . something indistinguishable.

THREE WEEKS.

You will do better to start on the coast. Or there is . . . mutter mutter.

PRENJ.

But now the railway is there. It is not what it was. They say the bears and wolves are gone already. He shrugged. This is progress, we are told.

Dr. Lakić underestimates us, said Dottie later, as they dined on lamb stewed with berenginas and a red wine considerably younger than the lamb. We are scientists.

Men will try to tell one what to do, said Prue. On that at least one can rely. She stabbed a piece of meat. That if nothing else.

Was Prue going to keep raking over Mr. Jolley's ashes for the whole trip? Dottie wondered.

But then there is the lateness of the season, she said aloud. It would be tiresome to find nothing on the wing yet. And there will be much of interest on the coast also.

Spalato

Arsenic, used in the vineyards to kill the phylloxera, had sent a chill breath over the land around. In the unnatural silence Dottie found four *Melanargia larissa*, just out of chrysalis, all of which she took, and some of the commoner southern species, but altogether it was disappointing. There was plenty of time, she reminded herself. They had barely started.

The streets of Spalato were littered with torsos, pedestals, capitals, chunks of column, as if the Romans had done a bunk in the night, taking only their infants and their greyhounds, and the Dalmatians had moved in without troubling to tidy up first. Dottie picked her way carefully, while Prue rattled on about Mr. Jolley in a most wearying fashion.

You wouldn't think it now, but I was a fine figure of a woman once. Edwin used to say . . . a young Athena . . . in Greece. When was that? '79? '80? I could have . . .

If Prue put half this energy into her collecting, Dottie thought, she would be lauded through Europe.

Work can be a great banisher of dark thoughts, she said aloud. I wonder if you saw Hamel's piece on albinism?

Prue's plaint ran on, holes in it where Dottie was concentrating on her feet.

The Attic climate, my word . . . jealousy of the gods . . . such a pity . . . wither and crumple before . . . twice punished . . .

They finally located the taverna Prue remembered from a previous trip. Prue greeted the proprietor as if she had seen him just yesterday and said they were in need of reviving. After glasses of something strong and tawny (a ladies' drink, they were told) and a dinner of green beans and hashed mutton, she was sufficiently restored to share her dissatisfaction, in two or three languages, with anyone who would listen.

In the myths it is always the young who die of love. Changed to various forms indeed. Flowers and trees and rocks and nightingales. Can the old not yearn? Do they not know passion?

We have an early start tomorrow, Dottie said.

Of course you have your children. It's different for you.

Was it? Dottie had become aware of an expectation, among her family and acquaintance, that she must soon cease her explorations, physical or even mental, that she would perch in a corner of Ralph and Netta's drawing room and interfere with the running of the house. It seemed unimaginable.

Ragusa

The walls shone gold by night and white by day. Rocky islands pinned the corners of the blue sky to the bluer sea.

They took a boat to Lacroma but found only some unremarkable browns and fritillaries. Probably the monks had been out early, bagging anything of interest. Much more rewarding was the Valle d'Ombre, a basin of light, its shores scented of pine and bay and caramel. The scrub crackled underfoot and the cicadas were as loud as the coppersmiths of Sarajevo. Ants, almost an inch long, ran back and forth and in circles. Dottie took fourteen *Gegenes nostrodamus*, twelve of which she kept, two over-wintered *Macroglossum croatica* (she allowed Prue to stumble across a third, somewhat damaged), and fine single specimens of both *Spialia orbifer* and *Pyrgus sidae*.

Their stay was spoiled only by marble pavements, glassy as the iced February streets Dottie had run up and down, with impossible agility, as a child. Now she inched and shuffled, but even so, on the third day, stepping awkwardly, she slid two paces and fell with such force she feared for a moment she had broken her hip, but she had only bruised herself and cricked her ankle.

You must see a doctor, said Prue. These things get worse if not treated promptly. Take it from me. I've been travelling longer than you.

Two years longer, said Dottie.

Still, said Prue. Two years' more experience.

And I'm a year younger, said Dottie, lacing her boot as tight as she could. If we're counting.

There would be plenty of time in the grave, she thought, for tending to minor injuries.

Cattaro

They had engaged the services of two moustached men, Vasili and Mirko, and a boy, Mirko's nephew, who would help with the ponies and the mule. The men waited for them outside the town gate, rifles on their shoulders, pistols and knives tucked into their belts and their saddlebags. Vasili was tall and Mirko was less tall, but still a foot taller than Dottie.

Very dashing, said Prue, rather loudly.

The track had outlasted a dozen empires. It crawled up and up and up. Also down and down and down. They were going one way and the whole population of Montenegro was going the other, with their chickens and goats and pigs and bullocks.

Dottie had no fear of heights, but as she swayed and swung above the many-footed traffic, the air lurched about her, threatening to conspire with its old friend gravity to send her fluttering down to the roofs of Cattaro far below. She looked straight between the pony's ears and tried not to think.

Prue, who had been born in the saddle, had followed some of the finest hunts in England, found the whole thing a lark and took the opportunity to recount some of her adventures.

I had such times in the Levant, she shouted. Did I tell you about my least favourite camel?

Cetinje

The royal capital was dwarfed by limestone mountains that seemed to have risen around it suddenly, brushing themselves free of anything as ordinary as trees.

The hotel was tolerable enough. They used it as their base, making excursions as far as Podgoritza and Scutari, where Dottie took three *Chrysophanus dispar var rutilus*, bright as Christmas windows, causing her to regret, yet again, that she had not even seen the British species, gone extinct while she was fretting about her children's schooling. Close to Cetinje, far from its usual habitat, she took a single *Thais polyxena var ochracea*, something of a prize, if not in particularly good condition.

Dottie herself was not in particularly good condition. She was still limping from her fall in Ragusa and had a bruise the size of Dalmatia on her thigh. The pain radiated to her hip at night. By day, when she ran with the net, it made her clumsy. Her vision seemed no worse but no better either. She felt it more in the early mornings—it improved with the sun, as the butterflies did.

A letter from Mr. Jolley had reached Prue at the hotel. She had not shared its contents with Dottie, but her renewed gloom suggested his matters were still important.

An invitation to dine at the palace perked Prue up. Quite right too! she said several times. My uncle being who he is. Of course, they could hardly leave you out.

Dottie unfolded the folding hat that she had brought with her in case of such occasions, ate the excellent lamb (roast, with French-style accompaniments) at a table laid with Manchester cottons and Sheffield steel, endured civilised conversation, as much as she could hear, about education, freedom, the fine characteristics of various European peoples, most particularly the Montenegrins, all the time wishing she was mixing poisons, studying her reference books, preparing the killing jar.

Before they left Cetinje, the local captain of gendarmes tried to dissuade them from proceeding, telling much the same tale as they had heard already, reprisals, tension, closures. It was not just the danger, he said, bowing. Some people, not him, naturally, might be suspicious of their motives. With apologies. Gracious ladies.

Dottie showed him the travel box in which she stored her finds, folded wingtip to wingtip and slipped into triangular envelopes.

This is our work, said Dottie. We know nothing of politics.

A scent of naphthalene curled up from among the small corpses and felt its way about the room. The captain turned his head away.

They were obliged to accept the company of two gendarmes, nearly as tall as Vasili and even more fiercely armed and accoutred, to protect them or perhaps to spy on them. The elder had a deep scar across his face, a badge that made everyone, even Vasili, defer to him.

Across Montenegro

As they rode away from Cetinje, rain began to fall and did not stop for some time. On the second day it was so torrential that for all they saw of their surroundings they might as well have been hacking through Hyde Park. It soaked their clothes and their bedding and ruined the dry food and any hope of butter-flies. Dottie's joints ached, her fingers were numb. She longed for basins of hot water and lavender in which to steep her hands. For the first time, she began to wonder if their itinerary might be ambitious for ladies of sixty-nine and seventy. Everyone was peevish. Mirko shouted at his nephew, who dissolved into unpatriotic tears. Prue snapped at Vasili, who said nothing, but only stared down at her from the vantage of his great height, then rode on so far in front that if danger had arrived they would have had to send a messenger after him. The animals were miserable too. When Mirko wasn't looking, Dottie had been feeding her pony raisins and damp corners of black bread and now, whenever they stopped, it nosed her hands and her pockets, then sighed and buried its head against her shoulder like a dog she had had once that did not like to get its ears wet.

And this was the best, she had to remind herself, the best days of her life. After this there would be only committees and fetes and recounting anecdotes to her fidgeting grandchildren.

On the third day, picking their way across rocky terrain, they encountered, as everyone had promised they would, trouble. A band of armed horsemen: insurgents or bandits or smug-glers. Or perhaps just local hunters. They seemed to explode out of the very earth itself, surrounding the small party in an instant. Everyone looked at everyone else with astonishment, and those with weapons put their hands on them but did not point them. There were seven or eight, moustaches untrimmed, faces unwashed, their clothes a hotchpotch of military coats and sheepskin jackets, leather boots and embroidered gaiters, caps and berets and fezes.

A bearded man in a Russian-style fur hat addressed himself in his native language to Vasili, but it was Dottie who answered, in English.

We are scientists, she said. Researching the lepidoptera of your country.

The men tilted their heads in a way that indicated they understood either the words or the concept but not both. Dottie continued, expanding on certain themes to suit her audience.

Montenegro has some of the most interesting butterflies of Europe. So little studied. A natural inheritance that should be celebrated. Something for all Montenegrins to be proud of. Something the scientific world should know. The whole world should know.

There was some nodding and a hum of approval. The horses began to shake their heads and chew at their bits. One or two took the opportunity to test the fibrous vegetation at their feet.

Dottie launched into the introduction to the paper she hoped to publish in the *Record of Variation*: the mountains forming a natural barrier between east and west, the convergence of occidental and oriental species, prevalence of aberrations, etc., etc.

Her students had begun to look about, examine the darkening sky, tug at their horses' heads. A man in a red waistcoat was talking in a low voice to Mirko, who was laughing.

The fur-hatted spokesman bowed to Dottie and Prue and said something to Vasili.

Be sure to tell everyone, Vasili translated, how we welcome our visitors in free Montenegro.

Then, with more bowing, the whole group set off over the perilous ground at a speed that seemed guaranteed to lame their horses.

My dear, said Prue. You were quite splendid.

Vasili grunted. It wasn't clear whether he was expressing approbation or disgust. He said only that they should move on before the rain returned.

Scientists must adapt and evolve, Dottie thought, just like other creatures, to their environment. Here, among ancient enmities and new uncertainties, a half-deaf half-blind elderly lady with arthritic knuckles and a limp might yet prove the fittest.

Durmitor

They pitched camp at 4,000 feet. The men slept in a shepherd's hut, dense with the aged essence of dung and cheese and tobacco but certainly warmer than the ladies' beds of fir boughs under canvas. When the sun went down the whole sky lifted away like a lid, exposing dizzy depths of space. In the mornings, frost bristled the pale mountain grass and a wafer of ice topped any standing water.

Dottie felt renewed. She did not fear slipping or falling as she crossed slopes of scree or balanced on narrow ledges. She did not fear the rumoured bears and lynxes, nor the wolves whose actual howling they heard more than once. In the evenings, when the party sat around the fire, the numberless stars seemed to look down on her with particular interest, as if they were beginning to remember her.

In her dreams she found herself at home, discussing menus or engagements, and when she woke with a start to what must be a spider, or worse, traversing her face, she felt only relief. The noises of the night crowded round. There was Prue snoring and there the ponies, rattling their halters and gossiping about who kept what in whose pockets. (Was this what it was like inside the chrysalis? she wondered. What did that hybrid organism understand of the outside world as its structures dissolved and reformed?) Desolate cries marked creatures butchering or being butchered. Anonymous creaks and stamps suggested that unknown armies crept to the bounds of the camp at night and stood watch over it.

As she explored the meadows and hollows and hidden tarns, Dottie found her new senses sharpening. Or perhaps the world was rearranging itself, magnifying its most important parts so that she might better apprehend them. She could see the birds testing the pitch of their songs against the sky. She could hear the breeze combing their feathers, and their heads angling to watch their prey. She could feel the plunge of hollow bone through air, the quick last pulse of vole or lizard. Proboscises scratched at flowers and nectar gurgled like a small pebbled stream. When the butterflies rose, their wings clapped applause, and they flew fat as partridges, right into her net.

The men let their guns lie idle, smoking and playing cards and drinking coffee. Mirko, who had always been the most cheerful of the escort, took to bursting into the songs of his country at all hours of day and night and had to be hushed sometimes after the ladies had retired. Vasili did not sing, but he looked out over the mountain proudly, as if he owned it, which in a sense he did.

Vasili is very handsome, said Prue. I dreamt about him last night.

He's younger than my son, Dottie said.

She did not mention that she had dreamt about the scarred gendarme. He had taken off his uniform to reveal her husband's smooth limbs, strong and straight as they had been half a century ago, when she was half a century younger.

Dottie took a *Coenonympha orientalis* at about 6,000 feet. That might be interesting enough for a passing mention in a journal. Prue took a very fresh *Colias myrmidone* from right under Dottie's nose.

Splendid, my dear, Dottie managed to say. A beautiful specimen.

All the same, Dr. Lakić had been right. The mountain was not yet quite awake. They needed to move on.

Tara

After a night of thunderstorms so fierce it seemed they would be shaken off the earth, they descended under blue skies. Butterflies crowded at fast-shrinking rain puddles. At Jabliak, they were obliged to accept another two armed men to accompany them to the Turkish frontier. With Vasili and Mirko and the gendarmes from Cetinje, their escort was now seven, counting the boy. It seemed an extravagant use of the country's resources. The men rode with their rifles ready across their pommels. But they chatted as they went, letting their horses pick the route.

They descended into the gorge through beech forest. The alternating shade and dazzle quite blinded Dottie. She had to trust the pony knew what it was doing. Shapes to the left and right might be trees or bandits or trolls. Even when they emerged into river meadows, her vision did not recover. She was tired, she told herself, after the loud sleepless night.

The men shot into the air to call the ferryman. He arrived with the unhurried assurance of his profession, entitled to the pennies from dead men's eyes. The ferry was three large tree trunks tied together. Dottie and Prue and the baggage were loaded onto it and hauled out across the dark water with no more precaution than if they were taking a hansom cab to Bond Street, while Vasili and Mirko endeavoured to remind the ponies and the affronted mule that they could swim. At this point all four Montenegrin officials said a brisk farewell and set off back along the gorge, not waiting to see if anyone drowned.

The reduced expedition made camp in a sheltered glade far enough from the gorge's sides to catch some late sun. Before nightfall, as if drawn by the grey wet smell of stewing mutton, two guards from the Turkish border post arrived to augment the party.

Along the border

They left their Turkish escort at the frontier, accepting two Bosnians in their place, to accompany them along the border and up the wooded lower slopes of a mountain where a butterfly might pass from one country to another several times an hour.

Dottie spent an unprecedented day in her tent and might have taken longer but for Prue returning to camp with tales of plenty and an unexpected *Polyommatus anteros*. It's the most splendid spot, she said. Such profusion.

Dottie reminded herself that she would be able to rest later. On the train. On the boat. Once she was home. There would be plenty of opportunity for idleness in her future. The next morning, they headed up to the heights together.

It was Prue who first drew Dottie's attention to it. An erebia, certainly, but which species? Its flight was more uncertain and meandering than any of the obvious contenders. Prue swung her net but missed and it was gone.

Half an hour later, Dottie was working the southern side of a meadow when she stumbled and almost fell. Looking down, she saw the obstacle that had waylaid her.

Prue was reclining on the softest bed of mountain grass threaded with cinquefoil and mouse-ear and thyme, but appeared in every way uncomfortable. Her face sagged rudely, like a person fallen asleep in public, and her skirts were disarrayed to reveal a crumple of legs. One arm was stretched in front of her, and there, its wings open to the sun, was the mysterious erebia.

Prue seemed unable to speak, but her eyes looked straight into Dottie's. Without need of consonants or even vowels she made herself quite plain. Catch it! she was saying. Isn't that why we are here? There's no time to waste—catch it! And Dottie did.

She was careful, dabbing chloroform on the insect's head and thorax before putting it in the killing jar. She made sure the jar was closed and safely stowed.

Only then did she turn her full attention to Prue. She placed the back of a hand on Prue's forehead, as she would have with one of her children.

Can you speak, dear? she asked. Can you move at all?

She unpinned her shawl and spread it over Prue. I'm going to fetch Vasili, she said. Perhaps they can get a pony up here. Or the mule. Or they could fashion a stretcher.

Prue made a sound that was not language, but once again, she made herself perfectly clear.

Prue did not want to be carried down the mountain. She did not want to end her life on a mule or in a Turkish frontier post or a Bosnian hut. If she must depart this world, she wanted to depart it with seeds in her hair and insect feet marching over her. She wanted to feed the worms and the plants and finally the butterflies themselves.

I plan to die with my boots on, is what Prue had always said.

I plan not to die, is what Dottie had always responded. Not quite yet anyway.

London

Dottie could still read and prepare her specimens. She could still see her children exchanging meaningful glances. But she had accepted that she would never go back to Europe, let alone visit Ceylon or Bolivia. Even travelling about the city on her own was difficult. And this would not be the end of her deterioration. One day the whole glittering world would fade.

The room was sunny, even in October, with French doors leading to a small, sheltered garden. Extravagantly flowered paper twined leaves and tendrils and buds and fanciful petals about the walls and porcelain songbirds perched on high shelves, tipping their heads to catch anything that moved below.

Prue could use her left arm a little, her right not at all. She could shuffle a step or two with help. She could respond to questions with sounds perhaps intended for words. Dottie thought she understood more than the nurses allowed. Prue had allegedly hit one of them with her stick, and her current attendants were burly women who did not seek out nuances of communication. One said, with her back to but in hearing of the patient, that loss of speech was a boon sent to ease the load of nurses, and Dottie felt like hitting the woman herself.

Dottie believed Prue welcomed her visits, although she often slept through them. On this occasion, Prue was awake, so Dottie shared a little news. She did not talk about Ralph's money troubles but she did mention her new great-granddaughter's fat cheerful limbs. She reported, without comment, on the latest troubles in the Balkans, spats whose causes she had not inquired into.

She asked Prue, as usual, if she would like to be read to, taking any reaction or lack of it as consent. She had selected, as usual, articles on calming, non-controversial topics, the macro-lepidoptera of Wychwood, possible double-broodedness in *Tortrix pronubana*, and as she read, Prue seemed to settle into her chair more comfortably, her breaths slowing.

When Prue fell asleep, Dottie sat for a while in silence, looking through the half-drawn curtains of her vision into the garden. A few late *Vanessa cardui* and *atalanta* flitted among the shrubs, rejecting this tired bloom, stopping briefly at that one, staggering as the breeze gusted. They would not make it to spring. They would be torn by storms and charred by frost and end their lives crawling, mouse food.

It would be kinder if they could go through one more metamorphosis before winter. If all that pearl and iridescence could be melted down and reshaped into something that would make better use of their last days: armour, fur, a gabardine cloak, sturdy legs, a magnifying glass, generosity, forbearance.

If Prue woke, Dottie would read to her again. She would take her good hand and the two of them would climb, deaf and blind and mute and slow, up through the pastures and sparsely wooded foothills, over the stony slopes wetted by infant streams, to the high meadows overspilling with flowers and butterflies, and that sunlit corner of the scientific record where their mark, Hawtrey and Sutton 1905, had been placed next to one species of erebia, a single bright fragment of nature's endlessly various, inexhaustible abundance.

Your Magic Summer

I T began with fracking and fasting, the superiority (unproven) of the life of action, and the raggedy-eared devils that scurry between the twin poles of rights and obligations. But it deteriorated. Duncan said, Because he's just some guy with his head up his fucking arse, and Carmen said, Grow up, and Duncan said, You grow up, and Carmen said, We are so finished, and Duncan said, You know what, we're fucking finished, like it was his idea. Then Carmen said, This is eroding my inner plane, and she picked up her bag (which had the tickets in it) and left. Before the door had even closed, Duncan had gone to the fridge for a beer. He drank it standing at the front window, watching people going out shopping or swimming or visiting friends or simply hanging about on the street laughing because the sun had put them in a good mood or maybe they were anyway. People untroubled by doubt about just how much they should be doing to stop the world burning and the new superstore from being built. Untroubled even about the tending of their inner frigging plane, whatever the fuck that was. When the bottle was empty he called Carmen and when her familiar ringtone sounded very close he turned, but it was only her phone, still lying on the chair where she had left it after texting her meditation coach, which was the thing, on the face of it, that had kicked off the row. He picked up the phone and threw it at the wall. Then he set off to find Carmen.

*

It had come to Lottie, first as an unspecific blurry optimism and then as a clear statement of intent, that today was the day on which she would go out into the world and claim the place it had been holding for her. She had only recently started feeling something like normal again after having been ill for months, nearly a year, with a mystery illness that the doctors couldn't seem to find a name for but had eventually managed to vanquish or at least keep at bay—she didn't know yet; it would be some time before she found out—with pills and enemas and EUAs and doses of antibiotics so terrifying that she had secretly stopped taking them, combined with essential oils and reflexology and a diet that excluded wheat and yeast and dairy and root vegetables and, in the end, almost everything except pears and poached chicken. When the doctors smiled their secret smiles at the reflexology (It won't do any harm, they said), Lottie decided not to tell them about the diet. But she believed it had saved her. She had read the internet from front to back and learned that food was full of all manner of toxins put there by the establishment for reasons of profit, not just from the insecticides and hormones and who knows what, but also from crops and cows that could tolerate the insecticides and hormones and who knows what. Lottie was a canary. The toxins that passed through other people like air stopped Lottie's throat and tumbled her off her perch. She was a warning of things to come, like those people sensitive to mobile phones, who had to line their rooms with tinfoil and wrap their heads in damp towels to sleep.

The illness and perhaps the diet had left her bird-thin and pale, her eyes ringed with lines like a map of precipitous terrain. Of course, that look was fashionable so mostly people told her how well she looked. And she could wear whatever she wanted, so it wasn't all bad.

On this particular day, the day of her finding her place in the world, she was wearing a new and skimpy summer dress—the sort of thing the grandmothers she had never known would certainly have tutted at—as she headed out, with her friend Bea, in search of celebration and commiseration.

Bea had recently broken up with her boyfriend, an Australian photographer who had promised, before he returned to Australia, that they would keep in touch by all the usual means until one of them got on an aeroplane. But now that he was in a different country, a different continent, actually a whole different hemisphere, Bruce had returned to the editing suite with all the passion he had previously frittered on Bea, and had told her (via Skype) that he regretted the time they had spent together. That was two weeks ago and yesterday Bea had said that she was over it. She had also said she and Lottie should go out and have some fun, God knows they both deserved it.

Yes you do, Lottie had said. You really do. We can dance away your troubles.

And yours, Bea had said.

But Lottie didn't think she had any troubles, they had all been killed off by the various orthodox and unorthodox treatments, so she had smiled and said nothing, reminding herself that Bea had just been dumped via Skype.

It was one of those days so hot that the city came to a stop: the cars stopped, the buses stopped, the clocks stopped, the copper wires and fibre optics in their dark, claggy tunnels under the tarmac stopped, the dogs and cats stretched out in the sun next to each other and slept, the birds crept into the deep shade of the browning leaves and trembled, and people spilled out into the streets, drinks in their hands and speakers around their necks, the air smelling of spice and tar and charred meat like a bazaar in Morocco.

Lottie had on enormous non-prescription sunglasses, protecting her from the day's dazzle but omitting much of its detail. She did not notice Duncan next to them in the queue until they reached the front and found themselves unable to go any further as he argued with the official charged with excluding the violently drunk and the dangerously stoned and, most especially, the ticketless from Your Magic Summer.

It's rectangular, Duncan was saying. The writing is green.

Yes, said the official. I know what they look like.

There's a dotted line on the left. There are terms and conditions on the back. In green.

If I can't punch it, said the official, it's not a ticket.

Can you believe this? Duncan appealed to Lottie and Bea.

He has a point, said Lottie.

Duncan narrowed his eyes to look at her, as if he was the short-sighted one. Lottie could make him out pretty well actually, because there were hundreds like him at Your Magic Summer. Short hair, a day or two's stubble, the long brown limbs of someone who did not work at a screen. Eyes pale as an empty sky. If you were describing him you could use *man* or *boy* and neither would seem right.

It was me that bought the tickets, Duncan said to Lottie. She didn't pay a penny.

Who didn't pay a penny? Bea asked.

My girlfriend, said Duncan, his pale eyes flicking to Bea for the first time.

At the news that Duncan had a girlfriend, Bea felt somewhat reassured, and Lottie felt something else.

Ex-girlfriend, that is, Duncan added. I suppose.

I'm going to have to ask you to step aside, sir, said the official. There are people with real tickets waiting.

Duncan shook his head at Lottie. Unbelievable.

Oh dear, she said.

Come on, he said. And Lottie and Bea followed him because it seemed unsociable to do anything else.

*

On the far side of the park, in the grounds of an old people's home, a thick, tangled hedge of hawthorn and bramble ran along the fence. If you ignored the PRIVATE PROPERTY signs and the stares of the elderly residents, variously disapproving, envious, confused, or vacant, as you ran across the lawn and pushed through the thorns, you would find yourself in a narrow but navigable space between hedge and fence, where it would quickly become apparent that the fence was not in as good nick as it could be. In this space, a discussion was taking place.

It's a couple of quid less, said Duncan. They won't even notice.

The money goes to charity, said Lottie.

Don't you ever do anything wrong? Duncan asked. Break the speed limit? Park on double yellows?

I can't drive, said Lottie, although the point she should have made was that no, she tried not to do anything wrong. Not if she could see the reason not to.

Civil disobedience, said Duncan. That's what closed down Greenham. Stopped the fourth runway. That's what will save the world from the bankers and the megacorps.

He was working with what looked like expertise to enlarge a gap at the bottom of the fence. On the other side of the fence was another tangle of thorn. From beyond it they could hear music and shouting.

I don't know how you think you'll find her, Bea said. There's thousands of people in there.

She's wearing red, said Duncan. And she's got a thing in her hair.

What do you mean, 'a thing'? asked Lottie.

I don't know, some kind of red thing, said Duncan.

The thing, Carmen could have told them, was only a hair clip topped with a red silk flower. Carmen believed, erroneously, that she had Spanish ancestry (her given name was, in point of fact, Jane) and took the red flower to be something that a flamenco dancer on a spiritual journey might wear to an event like Your Magic Summer.

But on that day, with the tide of summer brimming at its fullest point, half the girls were wearing red and almost every one of them wore a flower of red or yellow or orange in her hair. The whole park flamed with girls channelling their imaginary Spanish ancestry. Duncan would not, on this day, be reunited with his erstwhile love or the red dress that he remembered only because he had, earlier that day, before the quarrel, removed it. As it happened, Duncan would not see Carmen ever again, although he would hear about her, now and then, from friends or friends of friends, as she went her way and he went his.

That should be enough, said Duncan. Now we just wriggle through. Like foxes.

Like rabbits, said Lottie.

Like snakes, said Bea.

And so it was.

*

In the small, dark hours of the night, while Duncan's father, Rex, slept fitfully, muttering and cursing, Duncan's mother, Sheila, lay awake, as she so often did, enduring the darkness and the boneless things that came under cover of darkness to lie down beside her and stroke her hair and whisper sorrows in her ear. But tonight, as for several nights now, her sleep was disturbed by noises coming not from the darkness but from the roof space above it. First there was a heavy shuffling sound, like a very small man dragging himself along on his belly. Then a pause. Then a handful of glass beads, bouncing and rolling and scattering. Then an intent rhythmic scratching. It was not, she knew, scratching. That was teeth.

In the old house there had been a vast attic the whole width of the building. It had contained offcuts of carpet and ends of wallpaper, Lego, Meccano, stuffed animals with split necks and trailing limbs, trunks of summer clothes that had been put up there in autumn and never made it back down in spring, trunks of winter clothes, ditto and vice versa, empty fish tanks, empty hamster cages, empty birdcages, a microscope, a motorbike helmet, a sewing machine, photos and slides and cine film of people nobody could name. Things that might be useful, things that might be mended, and things that could never be used or mended but that had absorbed into themselves too much of the careful hope with which they had been acquired for anyone to be able to get rid of them. There had been mice in that attic, and birds had nested companionably in the eaves. The birds had chattered to the mice and the mice had chattered to the birds and all of them had chattered to Sheila like an ideal parliament, in which debate had finally shaken itself free from the sullen soil of language.

The new house was a charmless bungalow that had advertised itself as easy to manage. If you made the mistake of looking you could see the joins between ceiling and wall, wall and floor, wall and window, and the flimsy, temporary materials from which they all were constructed. It did not have an attic as such, just the roof space—*a crawl space*, the builder had called it, and at the time Sheila had wondered what that meant.

Was this a punishment? Sheila wondered, lying awake in the darkness. Was this what she deserved?

The next morning, Sheila waited until Rex folded the newspaper and took up his pen. It had been his habit, all their married life, to do the crossword before setting out to work or to play or, more recently, to journeying from room to room picking things up and putting them down again. Every day it took him longer to complete the crossword, so that now it usually took up his whole morning, and a couple of times this summer some of the solutions, Sheila could not help noticing as she was putting the paper in the recycling, had turned out to be words that weren't words at all. *Plahe. Bitnitw. Hqpa.*

She crossed her fingers against saucepans and knives and plastic bags and scissors and electricity, and got in the car. She drove towards town and then turned onto the ring road, a landmark-free corridor of roundabouts and big sheds, one of which would hold the solution to her problems.

She remembered when all this had been pasture and woodland and leafy lanes with names rubbed soft by use.

The lad at the counter, WAYNE, it said on his label, shook his head. I can't promise anything, he said. I can't say that'll do the job. Or that it won't. I can't say one way or the other.

The ads for the store emphasised that expert help was always available. Wayne did not strike Sheila as an expert. His training seemed largely to have left him with a reluctance to raise customers' expectations.

If you want to try it, you can, he said. I just can't make any promises.

You could check the website, he said. See what they recommend.

If it doesn't work, it probably isn't right, he suggested.

The device would project sonic waves (Sound, she thought, that was just a way of saying *sound*) intolerable to a whole ark of crawling creatures: squirrels, moles, ferrets, spiders, ants, termites, cockroaches. Do not, the packaging warned, use in the vicinity of guinea pigs or geckos. If that didn't work, there was bait (a way of saying *poison*). But she hoped not to have to use that. She would put her faith in the sonic waves that she herself, it had been made clear, would not be able to detect. Experience told her that it was usually easier to believe in something that could not be detected.

On her way to the car someone called her name. Pam from choir. Fancy seeing you here! Pam said with soprano excitability. What a surprise! Who'd have thought it! (As if they had unexpectedly run into each other in a forest in Borneo.)

Sheila had sung in that choir for years. She had left because, she had told them, her voice was no longer up to it. And of course you're so busy, they had said kindly.

I'm marvellous, you know me, always cheerful, said Pam, although Sheila hadn't asked. How's Rex?

She didn't know about Rex, then. Well, Sheila said.

And how's—hesitation, the familiar dip of the head—how's Duncan?

Very well, Sheila said, as she always did. He's with a lovely girl now, Carmen. (Carmen the sulky hippy, Sheila called her in private. Still, she must be doing Duncan some good. She'd stuck with him while he was away. Had she? Or was that another girl?) He's working as a builder. (Was he? After he got back he had struggled to find work. But he picked up enough odd jobs to keep him going. That and the money she and Rex gave him, kept giving him, despite their unease, despite everything.) He's doing very well.

Elijah next season, said Pam. You should come back for that.

Sheila thought of the great central aria. *It is enough; O Lord, now take away my life.* She couldn't remember what it was that Elijah was so miserable about. Perhaps I will, she said, knowing she wouldn't. Not unless some miracle happened. *There came a fiery chariot with fiery, fiery horses. And he went by a whirlwind to heaven.*

*

So are you living here now? said Bea.

Not exactly, said Lottie.

They were sitting at the back of Duncan's house on a square of pitted cement usually referred to, by Duncan and his housemates, as 'the patio'. Duncan wasn't there. Duncan had left in the middle of the night with a backpack containing sandwiches, tobacco, beer, and an unbreakable bicycle lock.

Lottie and Bea were arguing. It was too hot to put any effort into it, so they were arguing slowly, with their eyes closed and long pauses.

It's pretty much top of the what-not-to-look-for list, said Bea. Prison.

It's not like he's a criminal, said Lottie.

Breaking in is criminal.

An insect circled them with a discontented noise.

What if you were rescuing someone, said Lottie. Like, what if there was a fire and you had to break in to rescue a toddler?

Was he rescuing a toddler?

The insect landed on a flower and fell silent, burrowing.

Or a dog or a monkey, said Lottie.

What would a monkey be doing in a supermarket?

It wasn't a break-in, anyway. It was a protest.

In the pub the other night, Duncan had been talking about a friend of his who'd lived up a tree for a week and they'd laughed about it. Lottie brought up another of his friends, a man known as Long Terry, who had come to the house to borrow money and left with some printouts off the web and Duncan's camping stove. This was, in some way that Lottie could not understand, part of Long Terry's plan to destabilise the economy.

Shut up, Duncan had said.

What?

Shut the fuck up. Never talk about that. Never.

She'd thought for a second he was joking but he wouldn't talk to her afterwards. He kept looking round to see who was in the pub.

Sorry babe, he said finally. That's serious shit. You don't want to get involved.

You're involved.

Barely. I've never done anything. Nothing like that. Nothing at all. What have I ever done?

Quite enough, is what Lottie thought but didn't say.

Then later, when it seemed they'd stopped talking about it, Duncan suddenly said, What people forget is, it's a fucking life sentence, what he does. It's like being a priest or a lighthouse keeper or something. You can't just go home at the weekend.

The smoke of barbecues drifted across the gardens.

What about his girlfriend? said Bea.

Ex-girlfriend, said Lottie. She's some kind of Buddhist or something. I don't think they were suited.

Pigeons clapped their wings and cooed.

I really like him, said Lottie.

You always say that.

No, I really really like him.

It will end badly, said Bea.

You always say that.

*

Lottie had learned not to talk about the toxins. Too many times she had seen the secret smile come over people's faces. But when she told Duncan, he nodded and agreed.

I know exactly what you mean, babe, he said. They want to keep us passive. Drug us stupid with shopping and the internet.

This seemed to be a different point, but Lottie, grateful to be taken seriously, did not say so.

He supported her efforts to stay toxin-free, but did not always remember her rules. (Surely pizza doesn't count?)

One day he came home with a garden fork and a spade. We can live off the land, he said.

What land?

Duncan waved at the feral scrub beyond the patio. The garden, he said. Just needs a bit of clearing.

What had once been a lawn bordered by beds was now mostly weeds and a few leggy, bald shrubs. There was a loose, late-summer thatch over everything that fooled them into thinking it would be over quickly. But it wasn't. Duncan had to wrestle with roots, hew through stems, and hack at the ground, the spade turning as it hit stones and bricks and metal. He threw the rubbish to the other side of the path, where it began to form a pile larger than the space it had come from.

Lottie got cold and went inside. When Bea came round, they stood at the kitchen window watching Duncan work.

What can you even plant at this time of year? asked Bea.

Lottie had grown up in a flat in North London. He mentioned corn, she said. And tomatoes.

Tomatoes, said Bea. Well. Who knew?

One of Duncan's housemates came in. He had grey hair to his waist and every day he wore the same flared jeans with frayed hems and a pair of greyish sandals that showed his greyish toes. His hair suggested wisdom but his feet suggested he had lost touch with part of himself. He had been in prison too, Lottie had heard, although no one seemed sure why. From his appearance, he might have gone into a dark cell in 1969 and come out forty years later, blinking at the twenty-first-century sunshine like Rip van Winkle.

What are we looking at? said Rip, joining them by the window.

Duncan's planting vegetables, said Lottie.

Rip brought a tobacco tin from his pocket and took a joint out of it. The three of them smoked the joint and watched Duncan sweat. The pile of rubbish was nearly as tall as the fence.

I wonder if a spade is the best thing for this job, said Bea, after a while.

He'll need to put carpet down over that, said Rip, after another while. Let it rot.

He knows what he's doing, said Lottie. She hadn't seen Duncan work like this before.

Two days later, the plot was ready. Duncan had dug it over twice, removing most of the rubble and broken glass and the largest of the plant matter. He spent some time admiring the cleared ground.

Lottie read out the instructions from the backs of the packets while Duncan did the sowing.

A depth of fifteen millimetres, she read.

That bit doesn't matter, said Duncan.

Twenty centimetres apart.

They just put that stuff in for people who like rules, said Duncan.

Sow indoors in March or outside after all risk of frosts has passed.

It'll be fine, babe. Plants grow. That's what they do. Nature will take care of it.

He cut up an old crate to make labels, and Lottie wrote names on them and drew small pictures of the expected results.

As the weeks passed, Lottie and Duncan toured the vegetable patch regularly. Shoots began to emerge, green and white and yellow and reddish. They waited for them to turn into something recognisable.

The weather hasn't been on our side, said Duncan. He pulled up a pale, curling stem and turned it from side to side. What the fuck is this anyway? He threw it away. He kicked at something that looked like a thistle. Fuck this.

Lottie's labels continued to glow through the autumn with the promise of a harvest that she, at least, was still happy to believe would come. Perhaps in spring, according to nature's plan.

*

When Duncan had said *We*, Sheila had assumed he meant Carmen. But it was someone new, a doleful little thing, with all kinds of food fads, not allergic, something else. Intolerance? Sheila put them in the back bedroom, which she thought was the safest, the furthest from the crawl space and whatever dread things it now contained. There were too many flies in the house. The smell of death called to her all night. No one else seemed to notice. When she asked Lottie how she had slept, Lottie said, I was so tired, I don't even remember dreaming.

I didn't meet my dad until I was nine, Lottie was saying now. She seemed to be planning to sit in the kitchen the whole day, sipping hot water. (I don't drink coffee, she had said. Tea, oh yes—do you have ginkgo? Rooibos? Nettle? Hot water will be fine.)

As for Duncan, he had sweet-talked Sheila out of forty-two pounds, all the cash she had (Thanks ma, you're the best), and gone off to see old friends before Lottie got up. When will you be back? Sheila had asked. This afternoon, he had said. Probably. This evening anyway.

I thought he was dead, Lottie went on, still talking about her father. I don't know why. Turned out he'd been working in Nigeria.

I see, said Sheila. What a strange thing Lottie was. She was like a child still, although she must be Duncan's age. Was she really going to be enough to settle him?

My mum wouldn't see him. 'That Terrible Man', she called him. She sent me off on the Tube on my own to meet him.

They were all like children. They didn't seem to know how to get married or have a family or a career or even just a proper job. What was it Lottie did? Something about a charity. *Intermedia resources.* Sheila had no idea what that meant.

I thought I'd recognise him right away. Because he was my dad. But I didn't. I went up to this strange man and put my arms round him. My dad was at the other end of the platform.

Later, Sheila knew, tomorrow if not today, Duncan would ask them for money. Not forty-two pounds. Serious money. He would ask them in front of Lottie, so that it could not turn into an argument, shouting and swearing and crying, like the last time.

He had all these girlfriends. I hated them. I used to spit toffees into their handbags.

What kind of a name is Lottie? said Rex.

Lottie looked at him. There were three people in my class called Lottie, she said. I was Lottie Number Three.

Sheila had told her to ignore Rex, she was sure she had, but Lottie just kept answering him as if this was the sort of conversation she was used to.

Is she ill? Rex said. She looks ill.

I was ill, said Lottie. I'm better now. I think.

Never trust a skinny woman, said Rex.

Sheila took Lottie shopping with her. There was nothing in the house; Duncan hadn't thought to give her any warning. Every time Sheila put something in the trolley Lottie said, Actually, I can't eat that.

Why don't you pick out something you can eat, dear?

I'll just have some salad, said Lottie. So anyway, when my dad got remarried that was the worst. I mean, the worst until he died.

Lottie seemed determined to fill Sheila in on every piece of her family's dismal, ordinary history. As if Sheila would be able to sort it into some meaningful pattern.

Avril. She was my stepmother. I mean she still is, I suppose. His widow. Is she, or would that be my mum? My mum's still around but I don't see her.

I'm sorry, said Sheila. That must be very difficult for you.

I haven't for years. Not since I went to college. Before that really. When I chose to live with my dad and Avril. Which was a mistake, by the way. But my mum never forgave me.

Duncan's so lucky to have such a close family, Lottie said. It gives you an inner strength, doesn't it?

*

Lottie, who lived on basically two things, found Sheila's systematic quartering of the supermarket tiring. The journey down the night before had been tiring too. It had been a while since she had got tired like this. She didn't want to think about what it might mean.

Sheila said they would take the scenic route back. She pointed things out as they drove.

Some of the cows got out in the night, just here. A lorry ran into them. The driver survived. But they lost the cows. The vet had to come out to finish them off.

The old man wouldn't leave the house. His children used to come round with tins of food, but he didn't eat them. When he died, they found the tins stacked up around the bed.

My friend's daughter was in an accident here. The car turned over on this bend. Her face was covered in scars. Small ones. As if she'd fallen asleep against a fence.

There must have been other sights—castles, abbeys, locations of battle or revolution—but afterwards all Lottie remembered was this itinerary of disasters, and it was how she mapped the area in her head, so giving her an unexpected commonality with Sheila that, in their darker days, would stand them in good stead.

*

The day after Lottie told him she was pregnant, Duncan cycled over to Carmen's. He hadn't emailed her or texted her or phoned her. He hadn't been near her house, not once, not even just to look through the front windows. He'd kept away from mutual friends, places he knew she would be. He'd stopped trying to break into her Facebook page.

And Carmen hadn't got in touch with him, not to collect her no-longer-functioning phone and not for any other reason, either.

To Duncan, this carelessness for him and her phone seemed of a piece with how she had behaved when they were together, which, for all her inner fucking plane, was not always good. One time, for example, he'd come home early and found her in his bed with his friend Pete.

His bed! For fuck's sake.

He had forgiven her so many times that it had come to seem like the natural progression of a relationship. The relative tranquillity of what he had with Lottie sometimes struck him as a sign of its inferiority.

Duncan did not find it strange that he still thought about Carmen even while he lived (not exactly) with the now-pregnant Lottie. He saw no contradiction in it, and did not waste time trying to work out any kind of practical arrangement from which they could all benefit, Carmen moving into the house with them, say, and looking after the baby when he and Lottie needed a break.

The door was opened by one of Carmen's housemates, a stocky girl with a nose ring. Duncan couldn't remember her name. Hi, he said. Is Carmen in?

The girl looked him up and down. She's gone, she said. Her tone implied that all the bad things in the world since the dawn of time were Duncan's personal fault.

Do you know how long she'll be?

Gone, the girl said. Moved out. Moved away.

Moved? he said. Where? Maybe the girl would give him her new number. Or he could just cycle over. Or get a bus or a train. He wasn't sure how much cash he had. He could always hitch.

Nepal.

Nepal?

Yup. The girl looked very pleased with herself, like she had picked up Carmen, put her on her back, and carried her over the Himalayas all by herself. (Which side of the Himalayas was Nepal? He had no idea.)

What the fuck is she doing in Nepal?

She shrugged. You know that guru guy she's so keen on? I guess she's going to be like one of his disciples or whatever.

As he turned away, the last argument he'd had with Carmen, on the day of Your Magic Summer, came back to Duncan. So she'd done it. Had the courage of her convictions. Her fucking stupid convictions.

Duncan was aware that he was something of a hero to people in his circle. But the damage for which he had been jailed had been at best a mistake, at worst the work of someone else entirely. He didn't know. In the confusion of that day, the shouting and the kettling, the police horses like cliffs of muscle, people shoving and falling and running, he wasn't clear what had happened.

All he had ever really done for sure, in his life of political action, was shout. He went from one protest to the next: marched and shouted, stood in line and shouted, chained himself to something immovable and shouted, was cut free by the police and carried away, still shouting. Shout all you like, mate, the police would say. No one's listening.

*

Duncan had been running deliveries for a friend and had the van for the weekend. On the Saturday, he went off in it to see some people. He wouldn't tell Lottie who. He returned in the evening, gloomy and silent. He sat in the kitchen in the dark, smoking Rip's grass and drinking his way through all the beer in the fridge.

On the Sunday morning, early, he drove Lottie out into the country, to a place he knew. It's peaceful, he said to explain his choice. They walked up a hill and sat on a rustic bench (IN MEMORY OF BOB AND HILDA WHO LOVED THIS PLACE FOR 50 YEARS) with trees behind them, looking out over the landscape as the sun came up, big and pale. The first frost of the year had come in the night, and as the air warmed the trees began to drop their leaves all at once with a rapid, hissing pitter-patter like rain.

Charles, if it's a boy, said Lottie.

Charles? said Duncan. Charles? Are you serious?

It was my grandfather's name. I think. I never knew him. He might have been Charlie, I suppose. Or Chas.

Muddy, said Duncan.

What?

He turned her hand over and measured her long fingers against his own. He's going to play guitar. Play guitar and sing and never think of anything else. Muddy.

What if it's a girl?

Duncan shrugged. Muddy could do for a girl, too.

Lottie looked at the hedges and copses and streams dividing the landscape into manageable spaces. Spaces where people herded their sheep and walked their dogs and fished and spun and wove and collected herbs and berries. She thought of Rip and Long Terry and the mate Duncan was doing deliveries for, cash in hand. Do you think we could move to the country?

Why not? said Duncan. We can do anything, babe.

Near your mum and dad, perhaps.

The trees rained down their leaves.

When I was little, said Lottie, I really wanted a pony. It was silly of course, in London. But I wanted a pony and one of those little carts you put behind a pony.

A trap, said Duncan.

We could move to a smallholding. Get a wind generator. There'd be room for the pony.

And the guitars, said Duncan.

*

They took an unfamiliar route back through a new business park, quiet on a Sunday. They turned off on something that couldn't decide whether it was a road or a private driveway. There wasn't another vehicle to be seen.

Duncan pulled up at the kerb, put the brake on, and looked at her. Will you wait here for a minute, babe?

Why? she asked.

I have to take care of something.

Now? You have to take care of something at this very moment?

I'm leaving the engine running.

Lottie looked at the deserted buildings, with their neat-lettered signs, too small to read. What could you possibly need to take care of here?

I won't be long.

What if I asked you not to?

Just wait in the van and I'll be right back.

Lottie watched him walk along the pavement carrying his backpack in front of him. She thought of an orchard and a chicken house and a furry pony carrying a sturdy child dressed in jodhpurs and a hard hat, like something out of the Royal Family's childhood. She thought about lifting the sturdy child off the pony and packing it into a bus and leading it through a metal detector. Sitting across a reinforced-glass screen from Duncan. That's your daddy, she said to the child. Wave at your daddy.

Duncan looked back, not at her, but at invisible people on his heels, and then went around the corner of a building. This was, she would realise later, her last sight of him.

She did not wait even the minute he had asked. As soon as she could no longer see him, she slid over to the driver's seat. She had had three or four driving lessons when she was seventeen, giving up when she backed her stepmother's car into a wall.

Very, very slowly, at the head of a procession of cars sounding their horns and flashing their lights, she drove back to Duncan's house to pick up her things.

*

Again? said Sheila. What's wrong with you? Don't you know how to use birth control?

Lottie, who was unaware that Carmen had been pregnant last year, looked at Sheila blankly.

I don't know if it's stupidity or carelessness, said Sheila. I don't know which is worse.

Carmen used to wear the most extraordinary earrings. Extravagantly long, homemade perhaps, they brushed her collarbones and tinkled like far-off wind chimes. Such a lovely girl. They missed her. Although there'd been that annoying hippy-mystic stuff, of course. You couldn't choose your daughter-in-law. Or out-of-law. You couldn't choose your children and you couldn't choose their lives.

Done, said Rex.

Be quiet, Rex, said Sheila, as she never normally did.

They wouldn't tell me what they were looking for, said Lottie. That was what was so scary.

This was old news. She'd spent three hours talking about the police coming to her house, and only then had she thought to mention the pregnancy.

They made me sit in the kitchen the whole time, said Lottie. They wouldn't even talk to me.

The police had come here too. Gone all over the house. Put up a ladder and crawled through the crawl space. Come down filthy and shuddering like disillusioned estate agents.

I can't understand it, said Sheila. He can't just have disappeared.

I know, said Lottie. I don't understand it either.

Nobody understood it. That was plain.

He was happy about the baby, said Lottie. I mean, I thought he was.

Sheila shook her head. No sticking power, she said. She looked at Rex accusingly. You see? No sense of responsibility.

We were planning to move to the country, said Lottie. He had a name picked out.

Sellotape, said Rex.

What do you want from us? said Sheila. What do you think we can possibly give you?

Lottie looked at Sheila in her mournful way. They were all mournful, Duncan's girlfriends. He must appeal to mournful types.

I didn't know where else to go, Lottie said. I don't know where I am. I mean, I don't know where I'm going.

Her voice scratched. Her eyes wobbled. Rex held his left hand tightly in his right. *Plahe. Bitnitw. Hqpa.*

*

Sheila didn't like to think how often she'd gone running (walking quickly, anyway) round the avenues, up and down escalators, asking strangers if they'd seen a little girl. Lots of 'em, some wag would remark. The women were always kinder. Don't you worry, love, they would say, as if she was some mad old biddy, we'll find her. But this time Dipity was lost for only five minutes. Such a short time it barely counted. After every reunion, Sheila would buy sundaes, and while Dipity concentrated on building complex, doomed structures from wafers and melting ice cream, Sheila would talk to her about the importance of keeping secrets.

You don't need to tell everyone everything, she said now. Remember that.

Once upon a time there was a polar bear, said Dipity.

If I could pass on one piece of advice, that would be it.

Dipity frowned at her. I'm sorry, madam, there are no polar bears here today.

Sheila sighed. Where are the polar bears?

The ice melted and they all drowned.

I'm sure they didn't drown, dear. Polar bears can swim. Perhaps they just wanted a holiday in the sun.

Dipity looked at her sternly. They all drowned. The ice melted and they drowned.

You shouldn't worry so much, dear. Remember that. Actually, I think *that* should be my one piece of advice. Don't worry.

The mummies drowned and the daddies drowned and the babies drowned.

When I was a young woman, Sheila said, before I met your granddad even, we thought the world was about to end. It was all CND marches, ban the bomb, nuclear Armageddon, mutually assured destruction. Do you know what that is?

Now here are the tigers. Tigers cannot eat penguins, oh no, no.

I never went on a march myself. But people did. Your grand-dad did even, once or twice, before I knew him. And the world didn't end. No nuclear war, no army of radiated mutants, no ice age. Maybe those marches did some good. Who knows?

Sheila checked her phone. It had been off, she realised. But there were no messages. She sighed. Your mother has no sense of time, she said.

She would not say this to Lottie's face. In truth, she had come to admire Lottie. The way she had pulled herself together and taken responsibility for Dipity. Taken responsibility for Sheila even, in the bad times with Rex. All those ridiculous obsessions Lottie used to have. Now she just fretted over homework and teeth and the cost of children's shoes, like any sensible person.

And in another minute Dipity would be all grown and gone and Lottie would be lying awake conversing with the darkness.

It's gone in a blink, Sheila said. Remember that, dear. It's a ripple on the ocean.

Going down the escalator, holding Dipity's hand tightly, Sheila saw a familiar figure leaning on a pillar, watching them. Short hair, pale eyes, long brown limbs.

This was no surprise. She saw him everywhere. Sometimes, driving home, she'd see him five times in a row. As if during his long absence he had acquired superhero powers that allowed him to be in several places at once.

She had her theories, which she did not share with either Lottie or Dipity any more.

Someone had to save the world. Why shouldn't it be him?

She liked to think of him flying low over the countryside, his cloak rippling in his wake, dashing the baddies aside, hugging trees, and laying beneficent hands on voles and field mice.

You do what you can, she said to Dipity. And what you don't do, you won't have done. Remember that, dear.

The Earth,
Thy Great Exchequer,
Ready Lies

The companions

H M has been deceived by the dainty manners of first acquaintance, when Cassandra nibbled his fingers and blew nose kisses into his palm. Now she flattens her ears, twitches at the reins. Every hoof she sucks from the ground aims another clot of water at her rider. HM happens to know that horses, like all creatures intended to run for their lives, can observe their full compass round, so when she turns her head back, it is not to look but to make by-our-lady sure that he sees her look. Raindrops have beaded on her lashes and whiskers, transforming her into some frosted basilisk of the great northern ocean, risen to recite the charges against him.

Behind HM rides Shiers, also sulking, on a cow-hocked bay. Shiers has tunnelled deep into his habitual melancholy to uncover a seam of Stygian gloom. With every new set of accounts or assay report, his head has sunk further between his shoulders, threatening to reduce him to one of those nipple-eyed monsters of Ethiop. He may not even have understood the fine details. His mind is blunt, a maul at best, or a crowbar. For this reason, he

has been HM's most trusted employee but a tedious companion, rendered more so right now by a rheumatic affliction. He
sniffled and sneezed through a passable supper at the inn and
then again through a more doubtful breakfast. Aeolian fanfares
accompany their progress along the puddled track.

At the front of this small cavalcade rides the man who calls
himself Tall John, his feet dangling past the belly of a grey pony
that is first cousin to a sheep. Tall John wears a short hood or
perhaps a long hat of coney fur, which covers his neck and his
ears and merges around his face into a grizzled ruff where, HM
surmises, the coney stops and the man begins.

Since leaving the highway, they have slithered up and down
and around so many hills that they must have ridden six yards
for every one gained. Each ascent reveals more of the same—
bare, treeless wastes of sorrel and mauve, rainclouds tumbling
down their slopes like the smoke of burnt villages.

The bay slips, and Shiers curses. How much longer must we
wade through this by-our-lady swamp?

Pish! says HM, to assure anyone listening that in him, at
least, dwells the true spirit of an Adventurer. Pash! he adds,
more quietly, because perhaps Tall John, with his fur-coddled
ears, has not heard.

But Tall John looks back at them, with an expression that
suggests their exchange has disturbed the grasshoppers in his
head. A journey is as long as it is long, he says.

Indeed, agrees HM, noting that once again this could be
the wisdom of a rustic savant, the subtlety of a cozener, or the
rambling of a lunatic.

It was Shiers whom Tall John had approached first, with a tale that he could not be persuaded to elaborate or even repeat. When Shiers explained the finder's fee and its conditions, Tall John stipulated that HM must be of the preliminary party, plus Shiers, and no one else.

So here is HM, founding director and deputy governor of the Company of Mine Adventurers, former comptroller of the Middle Temple, former member of Parliament, knighted by His Royal Majesty King Charles II, in sodden garb on a sodden horse trailing through the sodden by-our-lady wilderness after either a simpleton or a crook.

It is clear to HM that Tall John belongs to that most disagreeable class of humanity, those who refuse honest employment, choosing instead to scrape a living off the land, like animals. They take anything they can eat or burn or sell: berries, acorns, bracken, scraps of fleece, leaves, peat, sand. They trap and fish, empty birds' nests, pull the very stones from the ground. And with all this, account themselves a second Adam, more free than a freeborn gentleman.

That morning, in the stable yard of the inn, Tall John observed the preparations in silence. HM still prickles from the smirk he spotted as he took up his reins. A look-at-you-fine-sir-in-your-fancy-sleeves-and-neckcloth smirk.

Smirk while you can, Mr. Coneyhead, HM thought. We'll see who is fine in the end.

Tall John looks back again, and HM sits up straighter, like one who has studied not only horsemanship but also fencing and archery (has Tall John studied fencing and archery? HM thinks not), and reminds himself that before getting mixed up with the Mine Adventurers he had single-handedly restored the fortunes of his wife's family and hauled the estate into the modern age. He has put occupation into the hands of the poor and gruel into the mouths of their young, even provided them with ministers and teachers at his own expense (that is, at the expense of the Company, but is that not the same thing, almost?).

He brings to mind, as he is wont to do in moments of doubt, his favourite poem, a lengthy ode on the subject of HM and his mineral pursuits (is there an ode to Tall John? again, HM thinks not), certain flattering lines of which he has committed to memory: 'a genius richer than the mines below', 'with virtues bless'd and happy counsels wise', 'commanding arts yet still acquiring more'.

It is comforting to remember, as the rain pools in the toes of his boots, that he is 'with virtues bless'd'. For it is common knowledge, among Adventurers as among rustics, that the signs they seek are reserved for the righteous.

HM wishes, above all, to be seen as righteous. Everything he has ever done has been for the good of his children, the nation, the deserving poor. It wounds him when his altruism is not acknowledged. When, instead of Thank you very much, HM, or HM has done a fine job, he must suffer, Where are the receipts? Where are the accounts, the evidence?

But if today's expedition finds nothing, then he has been cheated, and will look a fool. And there is nothing he hates more than to look a fool.

*

An unwelcome apprehension teases at the edge of HM's vision—a familiarity in the shape of the hills, in the contours of the valley through which their horses wind, and now a row of hovels, thatched like sties. With consternation, he realises they are approaching one of the Company's sites.

He has passed here once before, on a tour of inspection with Waller. It is among the smaller mines, not greatly different, at casual glance, from the surrounding dents and hollows and tumbles of rock. The entrance resembles a crude lair, clawed out by some night-skulking beast to evade a fiercer one.

A number of men and women and children are lolling about on the surface. They have the yellowed skin of subterranean creatures, and when they raise their heads it is with the single movement of a startled herd. HM tries to adopt a deputy-governorial posture but is conscious of how he must appear— mud-spattered, squelching, his entourage a blemmye, a sheep, and a coney-headed clown. He has a strong urge to retreat. But the opportunity has passed.

Once again he is to be tested. Not Hercules, not even Job himself, has had to overcome more obstacles.

Hardships of his early life—he achieves success

When his mother died, he mourned only a shade that had moved now and then across his sight, seeming always to be attending to someone more important. But four years later, he lost his sister, Louisa, who had petted him and carried him and played with him, teaching him his letters, helping him to fashion shiplets of paper and muskets of blackthorn.

What a blessing it wasn't one of the boys, said Aunt Verity, shaking dust from her little-used head, and HM said that he would happily trade, for Louisa's life, that of his elder brother Richard, whose preferred pastimes included kicking, smacking, tripping, pinching, and twisting.

He was beaten for this sentiment but did not recant.

HM's role was to be audience to the parade of his brother's talents. Richard was quick and strong and courageous. Richard was accomplished in Greek, Latin, rhetoric, ancient history, and the use of arms. Richard went up to university with a princely allowance and a small household to attend him.

HM, meanwhile, had to scrimp his way through Oxford and the Middle Temple on £80 a year. And it was not enough that he had to live like a pauper—his father denied requests for loans or expenses, even the necessities required to secure a royal appointment and thereby HM's legal career (not to mention pay off a number of debts).

In the end, however, he didn't need his father or his aunt or his brother or any of his weak-livered relatives, only his own industry and excellent judgement.

Mary was very young when he met her, pale and thin like her mother, with the same prominent bones. The family had made its money initially in salt, which might account for a certain redness, as if from crying, about all their eyes. Still, wise investors are tempted not by the sparkle of an object, but rather by its use. In her hair was the black of coal, in her irises, the grey of ore. She was the wealth of nature in the shape of a girl.

Mary was the sole heir to the mineral leases her grandfathers had bought up a century before and earlier, times so primitive that a man scratched what he could off the surface and then took himself to the next seam to repeat the process. HM's new family, despite their tenuous claim to nobility, had shown uncanny foresight, first in acquiring the leases, then in holding onto them as proceeds fell, and finally in preserving this girl, alone of all her dead sisters, for him, the most fitting man in the kingdom to exploit the opportunities of her inheritance. (What had HM's own grandfather left? His treasonous bones, to be, at the Restoration, removed from Westminster Abbey and thrown into a common grave.)

In the time it took Mary to produce three boys so very like their father that her part in the matter seemed negligible, and then pass away, HM had revived the neglected mines, turning £60 a year into £500. He toured the northern coalfields, where the latest technology was squeezing profit from land otherwise useless, and came back eager to introduce the ingenious new ideas he'd seen—gunpowder, engines of fire and water, systems of draining and ventilating.

But he found himself obstructed again, this time by his mother-in-law's new husband, one of those doddering curmudgeons stuck in the fifteenth century who thought gentlemen should not dirty their hands with commerce or anything else that he did not understand. Jealous of HM's success, he blocked plans for expansion, even further investment in the current concerns.

HM was in London when the news of this man's death arrived. In the privacy of his chamber, he danced a little jig (for the sake of his dear children). And when his mother-in-law wrote, begging him to return and take control of the estate, he allowed himself a hornpipe.

*

HM had seen, by then, that his ambitions had been too small and local—even a peasant could dig and sell. It was transformation and manufacture that generated real advantage. He set about creating what he liked to think of as a vast, modern machine of industry, his sundry projects like its cogs and levers, each fulfilling its own purpose while contributing to the functioning of the others, every part more profitable for its communication with the whole.

He blasted adits and sank shafts. He constructed horse gins. He renovated the abandoned smelting works, employing artists from the continent to prepare ponds and dams and engines of iron. He cut a dock and built floodgates, established battery mills, rolling mills, brickworks, manufactories.

Taking a lesson from the plantations, he imported men from other regions and bonded them to his service, shipped in convicts to work out their sentences. He was able to move labour between his concerns as required, so that no man need ever stand idle. Day and night, in shifts of eight hours, he mined and smelted and swadered and lantered and buffed. While the farmers still lazed in their beds, before even the rooster opened his eyes, HM worked.

Deep in the earth, he carved shining black streets of coal, lit with candles and drained of much of the water, ensuring his labourers were almost as comfortable below ground as above. He lined these streets with wooden rails, so that specially trained men could haul the coal to the shaft in great wagons bearing eighteen hundredweight. He laid more tracks between his mines and his works, his works and his docks, over highland and lowland, over (for all the squawking of envious neighbours) common land and public highways. To these surface wagons, he fitted sails. A horse could replace ten men, but a sail could replace even the horse. His terranauts skimmed over the skin of the earth, merry as a flock of small birds put to harness.

Master of earth, water, fire, and wind, HM schemed once again for expansion. The royal monopoly on silver had been lifted, and in the next county were rich ores—the wealth of three kingdoms, it was rumoured.

That was when it all started. Waller pouring poppy and poison in his ear. The founding of the Mine Adventurers. His present troubles.

An unpleasant encounter

HM recognises the foreman but is unable to recall his name. He prides himself on knowing such things, likes to think of his men as a kind of extended family, akin to lesser relations or servants, who roost and thrive in the spreading shelter of his generosity. (It is true that it is easier to think of them this way when they are at a distance.)

The foreman's memory proves quicker, and he greets HM with accurate deference. He seems unsurprised by the party's arrival, and reports, as if it were expected, on the progress of the work (Very good, says HM), the length of the drift (Very good), the quantity (so little?) of ore raised, the days of rain and the days of frost, the injured and the sick.

Very good, very good, says HM, nodding, as if he has ridden all this way in this foul by-our-lady weather to learn about Samuel David's leg or Edward Morgan's burns. He gathers the reins to move on but the foreman stops him.

If I may, sir, he says.

HM cannot think of anything in this wasteland so urgent as to give plausible excuse to leave.

The men, you understand, sir, are anxious. If there is anything you could tell us, sir?

There is no reason for anxiety, says HM.

We have heard talk, sir. Of closure. At this point the foreman—is his name Jennings?—looks at Tall John. Or sale.

Can he think that the coneyhead is here to invest? Are all these people simple?

Nothing runs faster than false rumour, says HM, with a memory of Latin and all the authority he can retrieve from beneath his dripping hat.

The yellow people, without seeming to move, have somehow crept closer.

Jennings is closer, too. So there is no truth in it? he says.

It can be hard, HM has found, to determine the sentiments of common men, lacking, as they do, the gestures and expressions of gentlefolk. At this moment, however, he has no difficulty in interpreting the glinting eyes and parted lips of the miners. This is the face of the mob at a dogfight or a baiting.

But they are on the ground and shoeless, and he is in the air and wearing boots, albeit wet.

Look at me, he says to Jennings. Do I look like someone who needs to sell?

Jennings drops his eyes and murmurs something that HM decides to take for an apology.

Perhaps, he says, you would be better served working than spreading gossip.

And with that, he jabs Cassandra in the ribs. Startled from a dream of carrots, she springs forward, all four feet leaving the ground at once, almost unseating HM, who hangs on by reins and mane and jabs her again for good measure. Summoning to his face the expression of a man who has studied horsemanship and fencing, he rides past the crowd, past Tall John, and on up the track. A trot, he decides, is an acceptable pace. A righteous man rarely needs to canter, but the importance of his affairs justifies a trot.

Soon enough Tall John catches up and jogs beside him (the grey pony judging its distance from Cassandra's bite), looking at HM like a schoolmaster awaiting the square of the hypotenuse.

Lead on, man, says HM. You know the path.

We all follow the path we have chosen, says Tall John, like a sage of bedlam. And he leers, showing all five teeth.

HM can think of no reply, and would give half his purse to put a wall between himself and Tall John at that moment.

This whole unfortunate incident, he adds to the list of things for which Waller is to blame.

An opportunity—the conspirators

His first meeting with Waller came about, it seemed at the time, by chance, when they found themselves in the same inn, one journeying north, the other south. Waller introduced himself, expounding in the most gratifying manner on HM's achievements and innovations, before progressing to the opportunities in that county. This was a new world for the new century now beginning, Waller said, a second Eden, a vast, untilled garden of minerals waiting to be cultivated by a man of wisdom and experience, a man of energy and insight, a man with the genius to raise the necessary capital.

It was a barbarous region, the natives without schooling, without speech almost, clothed in rags. The land was rock and fen and bog, not worth enclosing. The rain fell unceasingly, turning gullies to streams and streams to rivers, making marsh of every flat place.

But here thrifty nature had chosen to lay up her stores of silver and copper and lead, stacked and sealed and ready for use.

The numbers were beguiling. In the great mine that Waller compared to Potosí, the sun vein was eleven-foot wide, with seven foot six inches in ore, yielding more than fifty ounces of silver to the ton. The east vein was four-foot wide at its nar-rowest, and in places eight foot in solid ore. The bog vein, of potter's ore, was four-foot wide. There were further veins, each at least a yard wide, of silver lead, green copper (three tons of copper to every twenty of ore), and brown copper (five tons to every twenty).

And that was one mine of more than a score available for leasing.

Waller had calculated that in the first year, having drained the water from the main veins, fifty miners would raise one thousand tons. By the fifth year, eight hundred miners would raise sixteen thousand tons. The washed ore was merchandisable at 3s. and 7d. a ton. After subtracting the cost of bone ash, casks, candles, buckets, storage, and the mending of bellows, the lessees would clear an annual profit of £171,970 9s. 9d.

*

HM brought in his cousin and a number of other gentlemen with whom he had done business, and the Company of Mine Adventurers was formed. Like conspirators of less worthy causes, they exchanged letters and documents, met in inns and private rooms, the flames lighting their faces as they plotted ways to fund their enterprise.

A prospectus, one would say, advertising the benefits to the investor and to the nation.

Stating the portion to be set aside for charitable uses, another would add.

A plan of the mines.

Accounts to show their future value.

A lottery, said one—later they wouldn't remember who.

Lotteries were the entertainment of the age. The crowds flocked to them as to fairs and executions. The more distant the prize, the more certain they were of winning.

The Company would issue twenty-five thousand tickets. Prizewinners would receive shares. Those who drew blanks would be entitled, when the mines began to turn a profit, to their original outlays. There was no risk, no loss.

The Company advertised the scheme in newspapers and handbills. Subscribers included nobles and aldermen, a former Lord Mayor of London, a director of the East India Company, grocers, cobblers, widows and orphans, the poor of the village of Empingham. A fifth of the tickets were sold on the first day, all within two months.

And there, nature put her pert nose in the air and turned her back on them.

In this wild country, it was the dead work that was the problem: blasting, tunnelling, propping, draining, draining, always draining. Whole years were spent pumping water. Even the newest, most costly engines struggled. The floods always returned.

A little ore was raised here, a little there. But after the drilling and the draining, certain necessary payments to friends and accomplices, and such transfers and long-term loans as, having examined his conscience, HM judged himself entitled to (there were purchases required by his position: minor lordships, a second, very modest estate), there never seemed to be anything left to repay the investors.

He did what he could to put good news in place of bad. There is a difference between lying and presenting the best possible outcome. No reasonable man could call that fraud. But even HM was feeling queasy. He found himself pleading with Waller to somehow speed the works—employ more men, buy more engines, open more levels, any by-our-lady thing.

As the creditors started to bleat, the Adventurers conspired again. They made more shares and sold them to more shareholders. They borrowed money. They lent money. They set up their own bank to issue bills (hadn't the Goldsmiths and the Hollow Sword Blade Company done the same? hadn't the King himself when he needed money for war?), scant months before the Bank of England, like a jealous wife, seized all such activities for herself.

They were left with one bleak calculation. To raise ore required money. To raise money required ore.

He faces more troubles

The bay drops a forefoot in a hole, throws Shiers to the ground, and pulls up, trembling, on three legs. Shiers is only bruised and pettish, but the horse is useless and must be shot. It is decided that Shiers will follow the path back to the mine, where he can find some conveyance to the inn. HM will continue on alone. That is, with Tall John.

In the very moment they part company with Shiers, it seems to HM that the rain becomes wetter, the wilderness wilder, himself more mortal. He feels a greasy sweat beneath his cold clothes and wonders if he may have a touch of fever. He reminds himself again that he is an Adventurer, a genius richer than the mines below, knighted by His Royal Majesty, etcetera, etcetera.

As they climb again, the track fades into the surrounding thin tapestry of moss and sedge. Soon there is nothing more to see than the subtle byways left by savage creatures on their errands.

Long John marches ahead as if a line of beacons blazes before him, leading HM down a hill steep enough to cause both Cassandra and her rider to grunt, and along a valley where the marsh coalesces into a small river. Raindrops stipple the surface, reminding HM of the flies dancing at evening over the fishing pond on his father's estate, and then of the time Richard pushed him into that pond and ran home laughing. HM, green with duckweed, dripped slowly after him, intending to creep in unseen. But Richard had forethought him. Every member of the household who could be called from their duties was assembled to point and mock.

They ascend to a high plateau where reeds huddle in slaty pools. Cassandra's mood has become stoical, with a touch of resentment, like one of the less successful martyrs. When Tall John drops back to ride beside HM, she barely bothers to flick her tail.

The mare thinks herself too good for our paths, says Tall John.

This mare cost nearly thirty guineas, HM says (rounding up from twenty-two).

Tall John gives a fancy-gentlemen-and-their-fancy-horses shrug. The best servant is a trusty companion, he says. Spratt knows where to put his feet. Does not mind getting them wet.

HM glances at Spratt's woolly round flanks and decides not to pursue this topic. How much further is it?

The furthest point of the journey is its end.

And what is that in by-our-lady miles?

Have no fear, says Tall John. I have led other gentlemen to a just reward.

HM chews on this for a moment. A well-lived life is its own reward.

I've heard that in the city, merchants catch the rain before it falls to the ground. That the poor must pay for even the air in their streets.

What low people do in their muddy hollows is of no concern to me.

There may be mud on the highest mountain, says Tall John, and, before HM can assemble any kind of retort, moves on ahead, Spratt putting his wet feet wheresoever he chooses.

*

As they advance, the vegetation is transmuted to bronze and pewter, ochre and lead. Dwarfish worts and spurges drown in every hoofprint. Great plashy expanses of dark bog grass are topped with quivering white flags. If this is not the realm of goblins, nowhere is.

These goblins are well known among miners and Adventurers—the tapping of their hammers directs the listener to the vein. A modern man like HM may scoff at such superstitions, but the method is proven. It was shepherds following similar sounds that stumbled upon the Company's great mine, Waller's Potosí. There are many cues that a rustic is more fitted to detect than a gentleman. Underlying minerals influence the spring herbage, planting directions for those who live close to the ground. In winter, heat rising from the ore to the frost writes letters only the unlettered can read.

And HM needs to believe that, with or without the help of goblins, Tall John has made a find. Because even such ore as the Company has been able to raise is yielding a paltry four or five ounces a ton. Because the debts are thirty times the remaining capital. Because the creditors will not accept promises, pleas, or yet more shares, but, like overindulged children, demand everything right now. Because they are taking their case to Parliament. Because HM's defence is to lay the blame with Waller, who plotted from the beginning to cozen him. Because Waller has in his possession correspondence containing certain unwise statements that might, if made public, throw a poor light on HM's actions, on his knowledge and on what he has subsequently said about his actions and knowledge. That might, if taken in an ungenerous spirit, cast HM as unscrupulous, crooked, a liar, a thief, even. Because if he is found guilty, he may lose the Company, his sons' inheritance, his very freedom. For all these reasons it is essential that Tall John has located a seam of finest ore, right on the surface, fat and firm as floorboards.

The mist descends—the other realm

The rain has thickened to a dense curtain. If there is danger ahead, it will arrive without warning. Spratt seems eager to meet it, is speeding up, pulling away. HM spurs Cassandra, who for a few begrudging moments concedes a faster amble. (She will be ambling to market next week, HM vows.) The grey pony glides on, a two-headed centaur, round a ridge and out of sight.

When HM rounds the same ridge, he pulls up short. A few yards ahead, the land plummets into a great bowl of white mist. There is no sign of Tall John.

HM cannot see any path down into the bowl and is not keen to improvise one. He nudges Cassandra forward to take a closer look, but she digs her front feet in and, when he whips her on, wheels her rump around, stating that she has no intention of venturing that slope.

Halooo! he calls. And then again, Halooo!

Cassandra rolls an eye at him, pointing out that his shouts are as likely to attract wolves and footpads as Tall John.

They will reach you first, he says. All the same, he checks his pistol and regrets leaving the musket with Shiers.

He calls once more.

Tall John cannot be out of earshot already. This is some knavery. The man has tied cloths through the pony's harness, as tinkers do, and is creeping away, leaving HM to face an unknown peril.

The list of his enemies is long. Waller. Those in the Company who support Waller. The Company's creditors. Its rivals. The labourers. The ex-labourers. His envious neighbours, who, not content with digging up his wagonways, went so far once as to plot an attempt on his person.

He calls yet again, anger propelling his voice a little further.

It occurs to him then that perhaps he is misjudging Tall John. Perhaps the man has merely fallen to his death. Perhaps he and Spratt lie at the bottom of an abyss with broken necks.

The mist is surging over the ridge behind him, islanding him on this shelf like a mariner on a foreign shore, with only his wits to guard him from death or humiliation.

He listens. He hears Cassandra's breath, her creaking harness. The primitive croaking of a moorland bird that has never encountered music. Water seeping from every surface, oozing and dripping and trickling, and a gurgling like the laughter of small children setting nutshells to sail and watching them bob and founder. Grasses sighing, and beetles and worms crawling among the stems and burrowing down between them. Roots pushing into the thin soil and sliding around pebbles and rocks and seams and veins, knotting them in place, hoarding them, hiding them.

HM did not achieve his current position by sitting about waiting for deliverance. He has taken the 'paths before untrod'. It is his right and his destiny to enter nature's abode, 'the smiling offspring from her womb remove, and with her entrails glad the realms above'.

He points Cassandra towards the rim of the bowl and gives her such an almighty thwack that he loses his whip. For a moment it seems she will resist again, but she is too tired or bored, too habituated to complying with decisions from on high.

Down they go, through a white tunnel that leads to more white. The mist rolls and buffets, like a jeering crowd. The slope is steep and faced with loose, wet scree. The mare skids, recovers, skids again.

You must be kidding me, says Cassandra.

It is clear what has happened. Like those travellers of old tales who bargain with the devil, they have crossed to another realm, an enchanted, purgatorial kingdom where men babble and beasts speak, and time moves by inches. Outside, years pass, then centuries. Wars are fought, empires spread and contract, fortunes are lost and recovered. The world is changed utterly.

But HM knows how this future will be, for it is he who has moulded it. He can see it even now, through the billowing drapes of the mist.

His accusers are buried with their lawsuits in long-neglected graves. His sons and his sons' sons have nurtured his legacy through the generations and carried it to every corner of the land. Forests and pastures and all such wastes as they have passed through today are sown with mines and mills and workshops. Nature herself is employed to break open her treasury. No rock is too hard to breach, no material too elusive to extract. Her engines run day and night, needing only one man to oversee and perhaps a few boys to carry messages. Every valley, every mountain, every high street is lined with rails, carrying kettles and coins and candles from one side of the country to the other. Where wind is lacking, great bellows worked by lungs of fire blow into the canvas. Horses look out over stable doors to see themselves replaced, and wonder for their fate.

And where are the idle wastrels and the coneyheads? All such men are properly employed now, not in mines and fields, where nature's powers have supplanted them, but in counting houses and chanceries and stockrooms. Schools and libraries and coffeehouses have been built in every village and hamlet. Every manor house has its university. Even the poorest are provided with all the learning necessary to make them useful. In well-tended rows, they bow their heads to their tasks.

And past their windows, at the command of her masters, the earth's wealth flows. No longer curbed by whining investors or petty regulations, commerce runs swift and smooth and cease-less, unfeeling, untiring, a machine of perpetual and profitable motion. The rails gleam in the dawn like spiderwebs, and the song of gears drowns the birds. At night, the stars, the planets, the moon herself are dimmed by the glitter of furnaces.

*

Faint noises can be detected through the mist, and an enticing, almost familiar scent. Cassandra lifts her muzzle, cheered by the possibility that their destination may be near. She had a stableboy once who, in lieu of goodbye, gave her warm bran mash with cider and sliced apples, and ever since, she has hoped for such reward at the end of each journey. In her narrow skull, experience and speculation are pressed together, the days that have disappointed layered with those more frequent imaginary ones that have not, and compounded by increments into a single substance in which the main element is sweetened, hallucinatory mush. She lengthens her stride and hurries down the slope towards whatever lies ahead.

The following stories were previously published elsewhere:

'My Bonny' in *Zoetrope: All-Story* (2014)

'The Ground the Deck' in *Ploughshares* (2013)

'The Invisible' in *The BBC National Short Story Award 2019*

'Deep Shelter' in *Zoetrope: All-Story* (2018)

'Work' in *New Short Stories 3* (2009)

'Your Magic Summer' in *The Southern Review* (2014)

'The Earth, Thy Great Exchequer, Ready Lies' in *Zoetrope: All-Story* (2017) and subsequently in *The O. Henry Prize Stories* 2018

Acknowledgements

Thank you to the many people who have contributed in so many ways to this collection. Thank you for your wisdom, your encouragement, your expertise, your conversation, your cake, your puppies, your patience, your frankness, your kindness, your champagne, your ice, your ice cream, your iconoclasm, your words, your time, your fearlessness, your brilliance, your generosity. I am profoundly grateful.